HOUSE

of

CARDS

RENA BELL YEAGER

PIXLEY KNOB PRESS

Author's Note

House of Cards is a work of fiction, loosely based on the Biblical account of David and Bathsheba. The Bible does not give us all the details about their relationship, but it does provide us with a glimpse of their struggles as they deal with the aftermath of their affair. It is this struggle that is the basis for this book.

While there are no graphic depictions, the subject matter is of an adult nature. I have attempted to capture the choices we and others in our lives make, and the impact and consequences of those choices. Scenes containing adultery, betrayal, death, loss of a baby, and suicide may trigger a strong emotional response in some readers.

It is also a story of redemption and restoration. God's grace is offered to all, regardless of the choices we have made in our lives. Our happily-ever-after is extended to us through the forgiveness of Jesus, God incarnate, who died for our sins and was resurrected on the third day.

If you are looking for that hope, it is my prayer that you will find it in these pages.

Chapter One

The woman wasn't very discreet.

David Kingston looked down from his penthouse at the beautiful figure silhouetted behind the thin drapes of the condo next door. His hands in the pockets of his designer slacks, he smiled. The building was not as tall as his and only as far away as the two-lane city street between them. She had been giving him the same view every night for the past three months. Sometimes the drapes were closed, sometimes not, but the view was equally enticing. Of course, anyone from the two floors below him could see into her window as well, and was probably also enjoying the show.

One edge of the curtain moved away from the window frame, just enough that he could tell she was looking his way, as if she was searching. The soft glow of the light from a lamp somewhere nearby gave him just enough of a view to make the scene intriguing. She knew he was watching her, and she wanted him to. She smiled softly, pushing the curtain back even more to make clear eye contact, before closing them again. It was a bold move, one she had not made before tonight. The short glimpse beckoned to him, her eyes dark, and imploring.

David swallowed as he watched the woman. Turning away from his window, he picked up his phone from the dining table and tapped a quick message to his personal assistant. Who was this woman? What did she want? Why was she beguiling him intentionally? A man of his position had to be careful. Most women wanted money—or whatever money could buy. But the building next door was pricey, even compared to his. She clearly didn't need money. What was her game?

He left the desk and walked back to the window, sliding open the glass door to step out onto his terrace. New York City was lit up below him, the lights competing with the night stars above. The sounds of life coming from the streets distracted him for only a moment, until his eyes were once again drawn to the building next door. That was his building. One of many he owned here in the city. He would have known if someone new moved into the penthouse. Right?

Then again, he had people to manage the sales and rentals, among other endeavors. An entire corporation taking up the seventy-third floor of One World Trade Center. Many transactions came and went without his signature. He was mostly interested in the bottom line.

He blinked and focused once again. The woman's windows were now dark, and he thought she had probably retired for the night. After all, the clock was pushing midnight. He knew he should also get some sleep, but he was intrigued by her. He had not dated in a long time, focusing instead on his business. It was only natural to be interested.

A shadow crossed the tiled deck to the small rooftop pool. He watched, mesmerized, as she stood briefly next to the heated swirl of water before her eyes turned toward him again, her face illuminated by the underwater lights. She raised her eyebrow with a slight smile, dropped her robe, and slipped into the liquid. Was he seeing things?

He nodded slowly in her direction to acknowledge her silent invitation. Then he slipped back into his own home and sent another message to his assistant. He had to meet this nymph in person. Soon.

———

David walked into his office the next morning, the view from the tallest building in America barely registering in his mind as he passed by his assistant's desk.

"Good morning, William."

"Good morning, sir. I have that information you asked about last night."

"Great. My office, ten minutes." He glanced briefly at a closed folder sitting on William's desk and headed straight to his large corner office. Ignoring the view through the windows that spanned two sides, he sat at his desk that faced the open door and powered up his laptop, anticipating his assistant's report.

William entered ten minutes later, a folder in one hand, the other holding a steaming cup of black coffee. Nothing frou-frou for David. He was a tell-it-like-it-is guy, and he liked his coffee the same way. William set the cup down on David's desk, placing it on the coaster with the handle perfectly aligned the way he always wanted it.

David reached for the folder, opened it, and perused the top few lines, raising his brows as he did. He didn't like surprises, but this folder held one.

"Explain?" He looked up at William.

"The condo was purchased by your vice president of foreign acquisitions four months ago. His wife wanted to be closer to the heart of the city while he was traveling. Which he does rather extensively, as you know." William looked over his black-rimmed glasses.

"Where is Yuri now?" David sifted through the pages in the report.

"Italy, where he just closed a deal, and on his way to England tomorrow, where he will investigate more properties."

"How long will he be gone?"

"Depends on negotiations, but probably a couple of weeks. Up to a month, if he follows his normal patterns." William removed his glasses as he stood, waiting further instructions.

"Send her an invitation. Something elegant. To a private gathering at my place, this Friday." David smiled and handed the folder back to William.

"Sir?" The assistant quirked an eyebrow.

"Normal catering, dinner, and a light dessert."

"Will anyone else be joining?" William frowned and made a note on his phone.

David smiled again and shook his head. "No. Thank you, William. Nice job. That will be all."

William glanced over his shoulder once as he returned to his desk. David ignored it.

He tapped his pen on his desk, a nagging feeling in his chest. His Kingston Holdings mission statement was from Psalms 127. "Unless the Lord builds the house, they labor in vain who build it." Real estate was a billion-dollar business in New York City, and David built his company with a promise that each deal would be made with the utmost integrity. His dealings allowed him to diversify into other business entities as well, with subsidiaries and investments around the world. His business partners and clients respected him. He could close a deal with a handshake, and nobody questioned his intentions.

Maybe they should.

He thought about the woman next door and the invitation he had just requested. She was beautiful. Vibrant. And apparently starved for attention. Would it be so wrong to spend a nice evening entertaining her with dinner and conversation? He was her neighbor, after all. It would be courteous. Yuri would appreciate the effort to make her feel welcomed.

Decision made, he put down his pen and turned to his laptop. It was time to get to work. Friday would come soon enough, and he would put all thoughts of the woman aside until then. Or maybe tonight, he would see her in her window again and raise a glass of champagne toward her.

———

Elizabeth stared at the invitation in her hand. It had been hand-delivered to her by special courier three days ago. Gold foil lined the off-white envelope, the flap embossed with the Kingston logo. Her name was written in elegant calligraphy on the front, and the card was also embossed on the front, lower right corner. It was simple and classy. She had replied immediately.

She was invited to a private gathering with David Kingston, the most eligible bachelor in New York. Her hands shook as she slid her fingers over the classic woven linen, a base drum beating loudly in her chest. She had read the invitation several times since receiving it. Her conscience battled with her dreams as she considered the purpose behind the summons. Would it be a dinner party? Who were the other guests? Did he include her because Yuri was traveling so much? Or was it something more? She sniffed the invitation, noticing the slight hint of cologne. Was it his? Surely he wouldn't address his own invitations. She clutched the paper to her chest, her mind pondering as she prepared for the night ahead.

The last few weeks had been like a game of cat and mouse. He was over there, and she was over here. She had watched him often as he stared at her from his own windows. Night after night, he was there in his penthouse, luring her with his captivating presence. When she decided to slip into her pool, a quick glance at his terrace told her he was there. It was fun to see his eyes go wide as she slipped off her robe.

The bored housewife told herself it was all very innocent as she taunted the man next door. Oh, she knew who he was. CEO of the largest real estate company in the city. His face often graced the cover of business and entertainment magazines that came to her apartment weekly. Piercing blue eyes that held both confidence and secrets stared at the reader from the glossy pages. The same eyes that stared at her across the street, from his rooftop to hers.

Her husband had risen very quickly through the corporate ranks at Kingston Holdings, and now spent more time buying up properties for the man than he did by her side. She barely saw him a couple of days a month, choosing to stay home rather than jet-setting with him to barren places, which left her lonely. Was she sorry she had married him? No, but sometimes she wished their lives were different.

Was it so wrong to answer the invitation? It didn't mention the purpose of the gathering, but she assumed there would be several couples and others in attendance. Yuri was busy in business negotiations somewhere over in Europe. She deserved a little fun.

Elizabeth drew her silk wrap around her body as she left her condominium, thinking she should have worn something warmer. She looked both ways before crossing the street between the buildings. The action was as much to make sure no one was looking as to watch for passing cars. Her spiked heels clicked against the pavement, and she hurried as the light changed from Walk to Don't Walk.

The invitation contained an elevator code. She entered the numbers on the keypad of the express elevator, knowing the service only went to the top. The interior was decorated in gray, diamond patterned steel, and the panel held a single button labeled *P*. She steadied herself against the wall as it started its rise to the top floor and thought nervously about the invitation. Looking at her reflection in the polished steel, she wondered what to expect from this occasion.

"Hello, Mr. Kingston. Thank you for inviting me to your dinner party." She practiced in the elevator, her fingers flitting through her long black hair as the car rose rapidly to the top.

A ding sounded overhead, and the doors opened to a small foyer with a set of white paneled doors on the other end. The white doors opened as she reached them, revealing the man who drew her attention from his own rooftop. He grinned lazily as he scanned her figure, his blue eyes inviting.

"Welcome, Elizabeth. I'm so glad you could join me."

Words left her and her breath stalled. The man was gorgeous. Standing face to face with him, she started to second-guess herself and turn until his hand touched her elbow. He was dressed in a charcoal gray suit, his dark wavy hair hanging over his forehead like it refused to be tamed. His eyes perused her slowly, shining in appreciation. His cologne was subtle, and she knew it had to be expensive.

She was glad she had purchased her new dress. It dipped, split, and clung in all the right places. Her fingers clutched the wrap around her, suddenly aware of all the dress revealed.

She took three steps into the large apartment, glancing around as she did. It was decorated simply in neutral colors—varying shades of gray with accents in red. The doors opened straight into the living space, which was open and larger than she expected. A light gray leather sofa combo surrounded a steel and glass coffee table. On the other side of the room, just ahead on her left, was a wet bar filled with a variety of decorative decanters. Did he have any housekeeping staff? If so, they were staying well hidden.

"Thank you for inviting me. Am I the first to arrive?"

"It is just the two of us tonight."

She felt his hand on her back as he guided her across the marble floor to the large steel-and-glass dining table, which stood in the corners between the windows overlooking one street and the terrace that faced hers. A hallway to the left of the bar led back farther into the apartment. Taking her wrap, he draped it over a leather chair, and a whiff of his cologne tickled her nose.

"Oh. I thought there would be others." The table was square and set with two places, one at the head and the other across the corner to his right. It was close. Intimate. Their knees would probably touch.

"I've seen you a few times on your rooftop. I thought it would be neighborly to say hello. I hope that doesn't bother you." The baritone words resonated something deep within her. David drew near again, his presence unnerving her.

"No, it doesn't. I appreciate the invitation." She shook her head and looked around again, wandering to the sliding glass doors that led out to the terrace before turning back to face the room.

It should bother her. She knew that. Her heart beat erratically in her chest, telling her this was all wrong. But she was interested in seeing how this evening would play out. What exactly did he have planned? Did he have any expectations other than a simple dinner with the wife of one of his valued employees? If he did, how would she respond?

God, why am I here? She didn't talk to Him much, but she threw up the mini prayer.

The view out his windows was amazing. Perfectly situated to watch her through her own windows. On her own terrace.

"You have a beautiful view up here." The Empire State Building was only a few blocks away. Tonight, it was lit in the colors of spring—green, white, and yellow.

He stepped up beside her, placing his hand on the small of her back, the warmth of his nearness spreading from her spine. "It's one of the best in the city, as you can see." He guided her back to the dining table. "Come on. Let's enjoy dinner. Then we can take in the view as we have a glass of wine."

Dinner was a simple fare of glazed salmon, salad, and steamed vegetables, with a light tiramisu for dessert. Elizabeth ate a few bites of each, watching him as she did. Conversation was mostly about benign subjects. The weather, books, her pet macaw. Candles flickered between them, casting shadows on the walls that held conversations of their own. Finally, they rose and took their wine to the terrace.

"David, why did you invite me here tonight?" Elizabeth spoke softly and turned to face him as they stood looking out over the city.

"You looked lonely. You know. When I saw you the other night." He pointed toward her terrace.

"You know I'm married." It wasn't a question. She let her eyes meet his as she ran her fingertip around the rim of her wine glass.

"Your husband is a lucky man. But where is he? He shouldn't be leaving his lovely wife alone. I certainly wouldn't." His voice was as smooth as warm butter. He leaned his back against the tall rail surrounding the concrete patio, one ankle crossed over the other, his eyes on hers.

"My husband—" she paused and took a sip—"is somewhere on

the other side of the world. Buying up property for you." She moved closer, watching him over her glass.

"He has teams that he can send out. He doesn't have to negotiate every deal himself."

She felt like they were in their own negotiations, and she hesitated before speaking again. She glanced back through the sliding terrace doors to the white-paneled set leading to the elevator. How many steps would it take to escape?

"You've been spending a lot of time on your rooftop." He stood, moving closer.

"And you've noticed." She took a deep breath to calm her nerves. She had never cheated on her husband. Never.

"Well, it is right next door." He pointed across the street with his glass before taking his own sip.

"Yes, the building has wonderful amenities. More than expected, including the view." She knew how to play coy, and her body took over while her brain and heart warred within her. She set her glass on a nearby table and moved close enough to lay her hand on his chest. Her brain screamed at her to stop. Run away. Go home.

"My view is much better." He raised an eyebrow at her. "You've been teasing me for weeks." He set his glass down on the table, next to hers. The crystal rang as the glasses clinked. "You are teasing me now in that dress, with your lovely hand on my chest." He covered her hand with his, wrapping his fingers around hers.

She shivered as goosebumps rose along her arms. She wasn't sure what she expected to happen tonight, or what he was looking for. She loved Yuri. She was committed to him. But David was right. She was alone more often than not. And her game of cat and mouse was about to turn real. But was she the cat? Or the mouse?

———

David was mesmerized by the woman in front of him. The woman who was close enough to kiss, if he wanted to. The little black dress accentuated every curve and valley, and her touch was like velvet. His pulse raced under the heat of her fingers, and he lifted her hand to his lips.

He had only thought to invite her over for a pleasant evening of wine, a nice dinner, and a bit of conversation. But this vixen in front of him tore down every defense he could muster. Her long dark hair, dark eyes, and exotic beauty intoxicated him more than the wine ever could. Her slender form made a perfect silhouette behind her curtains, but now she stood before him, hiding nothing, and was perfectly proportioned to fit into his arms.

"David." Her breathy voice was soft, like the puffy clouds ahead of a looming storm. Her long lashes fluttered over dark eyes, reflecting the stars that hung overhead. But this wasn't the harmless flirtation of an inexperienced woman. It was a promise. A smoky, all-consuming siren call that told him she knew exactly what he wanted.

David hesitated. Was he really going to do this? He was a man of principle. Forthright and honest, like his namesake in the Bible. A man after God's own heart. But the temptation was too great, the urge unbearable. His vice president was thousands of miles away, and Elizabeth was here.

He lowered his head to hers and grazed her lips softly with his. She rose to meet him, and he teased her a second time, slowly sliding his hand down her back. Her lips were as warm and soft as he'd imagined they would be, and she answered his unspoken question. First, tentatively. Then more consuming. They moved together in a slow dance of passion as they continued to kiss and all doubt fled him. The terrace door opened as they drew near, then closed behind them.

The heat of the moment overtook his common sense. He knew he should stop, but he was too far gone. Her perfume made him see stars. Was that jasmine? It was a known aphrodisiac. He buried his nose in her neck and pushed her backward the final few feet, where they entered the room that held the secrets of the night.

Chapter Two

David entered his office the following Monday, impeccably dressed as always. Designer suit, crisp white shirt, red power tie. This was his domain, his world, and he built it.

His father sold real estate back home in Iowa, but those deals were mostly rural homes. Some farms sold for high dollars if there was a lot of acreage, and that was where David had gotten the bug. After business school, he immediately got his real estate license and helped his dad on some of the larger deals. Saved as much as he could. And used his savings and experience to become partner in a real estate company in New York. His business partner was also his mentor, and he quickly moved into the upper echelons until he finally bought the company out and sat on top at the age of forty-one.

Now he could look out over the city he had fought for from his office in One World Trade Center. The company occupied the entire forty-thousand square feet of the seventy-third floor, mostly because he didn't want intruders in his domain, the space a prize in the iconic building. The prismed shape provided a panoramic view of the city, the harbors, and New Jersey, and could be seen from miles away.

"Good morning, William." David smiled at his assistant as he sauntered into the office.

"Good morning, sir. You're in a good mood this morning. I trust your dinner party went well?"

"Better than expected. Send Ms. Yassin flowers. Something with jasmine in it."

William looked at David once, squinted, then quickly turned his head back to his computer. The man was a gem. He never questioned his boss and always came through. No matter the task.

David walked through the door to his inner office, then stopped and turned.

"Where is Yuri today?"

"England."

"Do we have any more properties he can look at while he is over there?" His conscience kicked him in the shin, but he ignored the nudge.

"There are a couple of possibilities in Scotland."

"Great. He might as well investigate those, too." An inner voice told him he was betraying his most loyal employee, but he shoved that thought aside.

"Certainly, sir. I'll send him a message today." William turned to his keyboard and shook his head slightly before sending the request.

David walked back into his office and shut the door. Sitting down at his desk, he checked his calendar for meetings. Then he opened his email and scanned his messages. He had lunch with his attorney and afternoon prep for a board meeting that was scheduled for next week. William would do most of the work, but David always wanted to review the numbers before meeting with his major partners. They expected return on their investment, too.

He had diversified as his empire grew, into medical, technology, and energy portfolios. He sat on multiple boards and enjoyed a great game of chess. He was David Kingston, and people bowed at his feet. Not literally, but in their minds and in business. No one would dare say "no" to him.

"Mr. Kingston?" William's calm voice spoke from the small intercom. "Mr. Yusavi is here to see you."

Antoni. David looked at the time on his laptop and realized he had a meeting with his friend that he had not put on his calendar. His door opened, and his mentor strode into the room.

"You are looking well, David. What put that smile on your face this morning? Was it the rally the stock market took at the opening bell? Made a few bucks, did you?"

"Come in, my friend. We both did well this morning." He pointed at the chair in front of his desk. "Let's talk about that possibility in the Middle East." They shook hands and took their respective seats. If Antoni wanted to believe his smile came from making a little money, that worked well for him.

———

Elizabeth pulled her black Italian silk robe around her body as she left her bedroom. The smell of perfectly blended coffee wafted down the hallway, guiding her nose. Her maid always arrived at six a.m., prepared a fresh fruit and pastry breakfast, orange juice, and her preferred coffee blend. The kitchen always sparkled. Not a dirty dish in sight, and the maid even opened the canvas cover over Pete's cage and fed the scarlet macaw his specialized birdseed, filling the glass feeder that hung from the side of the tall cage. She then left promptly at seven fifty-five. Five minutes before Elizabeth's alarm pulled her from sleep.

"Good morning." The colorful parrot repeated the words it was taught to say every morning, his brilliant rainbow feathers fluffing as he shifted back and forth on his perch. The giant creature was nearly three feet in length, his floor-to-ceiling cage taking up an entire section of the room in front of the sliding doors that led to the terrace. Yuri gave him to her when they moved into the building. He was a small source of comfort, since her husband traveled so much.

"Good morning, Pete." She went to her refrigerator, opened a box of diced pineapple, and fed a piece to him before popping another in her mouth. The large bird ate several pieces a day, in addition to his special parrot food.

A song from a show tune came to mind, and she sang a line, her voice off-key.

The bird sang in return, imitating her note for note.

Smiling at his off-key mimicry, she blew a kiss at the bird and sat down with her coffee.

Last night she slept better than she had in months. A smile crept across her face as she recalled her weekend with David. One small dinner had turned into forty-eight hours of bliss. If only her husband would treat her that way.

Her phone buzzed in a special pattern that she set for Yuri. She glanced at the text.

"I will be delayed again. I have two more properties to review before coming home."

Elizabeth sighed. This was nothing new. She spoke more to the bird than she did to her husband. While she knew Yuri's globe-trotting was his job and provided the income that allowed her to live so lavishly, she had no desire to travel like that. It was sometimes fun to visit, but after a few days here and there, she rapidly grew bored. She wished that he would delegate some of these trips. But he was a student at David's feet, even as a vice president. Elizabeth wondered if he would ever come home.

Two hours later, the doorbell rang. Looking through the peephole, she found a delivery man with a bouquet of flowers. She opened the door.

"Flowers for Ms. Yassin." The young man couldn't be more than nineteen or twenty and was likely working his way through school.

Elizabeth accepted the bouquet and started to hand him a twenty-dollar tip. He pushed the bill back into her hand.

"No need, ma'am. It's covered."

Okay. She might have to take back her thoughts about her husband. At least he sent flowers. She went to her dining table and sniffed the wrapped bundle before setting it down. It smelled like her perfume. Pulling back the tissue, she peeled the box away from the ornate vase and looked for the card.

"Friday night. Eight p.m. My place."

Her shoulders sagged in disappointment. It wasn't signed, but she knew it had to be from David, not her husband. And it wasn't an invitation. More of a royal summons. Well, he was king of his empire.

She rested her chin in her hand on the table and stared at the flowers, recalling their weekend together. She woke up Saturday morning to breakfast in bed. It was a full spread of eggs, waffles, pure maple syrup, fruit, and her special blend of coffee. How did he get that? Only her maid knew that recipe. They shared the meal, and his attention to her made it feel more like a honeymoon than an affair.

He was an incredibly handsome man. Wavy dark brown hair, tanned skin, and the bluest eyes she had ever seen. Muscles that wrapped around her in security and warmth, making her feel cherished. Legs like pillars.

They spent time in his hot tub. Another candlelight dinner where soft music played from hidden speakers. The gentle guitar and strings lulled her into staying another night. And oh, what a night it was.

What would he expect this Friday? What did he hope to accomplish from these meetings, other than the obvious? Maybe she should take a change of clothes with her this time. Maybe he would whisk her off somewhere, and they would do something fun. Or maybe he would tire of her quickly and toss her aside, just as her husband was doing. She shook her head. That was a lot of maybe.

It was rather presumptuous of David to assume that she would respond without question. She could say no. She should say no. A little voice in her head said *no, no, no*. But what was Yuri doing? Where were these new properties he had to investigate? She didn't even know where her husband was. When he left a month ago, he told her he was going to Europe. But where in Europe? Was it Spain? No, Italy? She should have gone with him.

"Pretty bird. Pretty bird. Good morning."

She stared at her feathered companion. He was happy in his cage, but she was not. The walls of her penthouse were constricting. She made her decision. Since Yuri would not be home for a while, she might as well have fun.

———

The flowers came again the next Monday. And the three Mondays after that. Each Friday, Elizabeth took the private elevator to David's apartment. He would open his door for her, and she would enter his domain, ignoring the elephant between them. Each weekend they spent forty-eight hours entangled in each other's arms. He provided her with her favorite meals. The finest chocolates. A beautiful robe and all her special toiletries. But every Sunday night he closed his door behind her, and she walked back across the street to her lonely home. Alone again.

Yuri had not returned. There was always one more property to look at. One more reason why he needed to be away from her arms. She wondered if he was spending his nights alone. Was he pouring expensive wine into a crystal glass for a beautiful woman, his eyes only for her? Did her dress hug every curve? Had she enticed him by skinny-dipping in a rooftop pool? Were they wrapped up in each other's arms, their hunger for company seasoned with the spice of wantonness?

Could anybody blame Elizabeth for seeking comfort with the man next door? She was a young woman, barely into her twenties. She didn't care if David had a little bit of gray at his temples. It made him look very distinguished.

She used the best skin care creams to retain her beauty, and she knew she was beautiful. One look from David told her that. But she wanted someone who would appreciate her every morning. And every night. She didn't want a weekend lover. She didn't need stress lines from worrying about where either relationship was going. And she didn't want to wake up one day and be a dried-up old woman with no man to keep her warm and only a bird for company.

Elizabeth picked up the silver frame holding their wedding picture from her nightstand. Yuri's gaze on hers as they stood arm in arm sparked a flame in her belly. The first couple years of their marriage was filled with passion. But then he met David and began his travels around the world, his work becoming his mistress. The emotional miles between them grew as they drifted farther apart.

She feathered her fingers across his face on the picture, his dark eyes holding a look she had not seen from him in a while. It was a look that promised they would be together forever.

Now, each trip took him farther away. As foreign acquisitions VP, he always traveled out of the United States. At first, his trips were short. Canada and Mexico were his destinations. Then their deals ventured into Central America. Currently he was traveling across Europe. Where would he go next? Asia? Africa? If he did that, how would she get her husband back?

She pitched her head back and groaned at the ceiling, fueling her ire before throwing the offending picture at the wall with a primal scream. It hit the television, causing both to crash to the floor. She slumped to her soft, exquisite mattress and curled into a ball. She enjoyed spending time with David. Just thinking of him made heat creep up her face. But he wasn't her husband. He wasn't Yuri.

Chapter Three

"I'm going out of town for a couple of weeks. And I'm bringing Yuri home."

David and Elizabeth sat in the wrought iron glider on the end of his terrace while the night's stars glowed overhead. The air up in the heights of the city was clear and crisp tonight. They were well into spring, but at this height there was still a hint of briskness in the air. He wrapped his arm around her, as he had every weekend for the past few weeks, but just as the seasons would change, he knew in his heart this affair would have to end. He needed to call Yuri home. His trusted employee may be as clueless as a bat when it came to his wife, but David couldn't continue to do this. It was a temporary fling, fun for a little while. But it had to stop.

"Yuri? He doesn't even know I exist." She crossed her arms, her posture mimicking the pout in her voice.

"He's your husband."

She turned toward David, eyes flashing. "You are more of a husband than he is."

David sighed. "This should never have happened, and you know it." He pointed his finger back and forth between them.

Elizabeth grabbed his hand again, squeezing his fingers. "So, you would use me and send me away? Mister Big Shot CEO who can have any woman he wants, takes another man's wife? Plays with her for a while then sends her home? You invited me here. Remember? I still have the invitation to prove it." She sounded furious, and David supposed she had a right to be. But he was not the only guilty one.

"Like you enticed me? With nighttime wanderings? Skinny-dipping in the pool that you clearly knew I had full view of?"

"I had on a bikini."

"What little of it there was."

"Well, now you have seen all of me, anyway. So, what does it matter?"

David stood in a huff and opened the terrace door to go back inside, his blue eyes turning to ice. "It matters a lot, Elizabeth. We shouldn't have done this. It is time for you to go home."

The woman was even more beautiful when she was angry. He didn't know why he had this sudden bout of moral consciousness. The awareness of their behavior. He could feel the fire flashing from her dark mahogany orbs, scorching his soul as she followed him into his suite.

"I have half a mind to tell Yuri what we've been doing." She stood with her arms crossed.

"He won't believe you."

"I suppose not. He's very loyal to you. More so than to his own wife."

This conversation was disintegrating rapidly, and her threat made him pause, his hand on the wet bar. How would Yuri respond if Elizabeth did tell him? Would he believe her? If so, he could lash out, doing substantial damage to David's international business. Some countries viewed women as nothing more than property. But along with that was the understanding that you didn't steal another man's wife. Unless you were a king. David rubbed the back of his neck. The longer this affair went on, the worse it would be. It had to stop now. He would not be blackmailed by Elizabeth or anyone else.

He walked straight to his white double paneled doors. He paid thousands for these doors, but they opened and closed just like any others. He tugged on the right side and looked back at Elizabeth, making his intentions clear.

She gathered up everything he had given her and stuffed it into a small bag, then headed for the door. She paused, her eyes glinting in thought. Going back into his kitchen, she pulled his kitchen shears from the knife block, then pulled the robe out of the bag and sliced through the collar before tearing the garment down the middle.

"What are you doing?" He narrowed his eyes together.

"Ripping you out of my heart. It's an old Jewish custom. It means you are dead to me." She stuffed the robe back into the bag and tossed the scissors on the granite counter. Then she opened the door under the kitchen sink and dropped the bag and its contents into the garbage can. And as she passed by his bar, she grabbed a cut crystal decanter and threw it at his sliding glass door, shattering the door and the decanter as amber liquid splashed and dripped to the floor, mingling with the shiny shards. Finally, she walked past him to the hallway leading to the elevator, holding her head high, regally exiting like a queen.

David shut the door, turned the lock, crossed the room, and sank into his sofa. Her actions shouted much louder than her words. And she had surprisingly good aim, with her words and with her arm. He would have to call someone to repair his door. He rubbed his hand over his face, scratched his neck, then moved his hand back up over his face and rubbed the back of his neck. What was he to do now?

That was harder than he expected it to be. When they started this affair, they both knew it was just a fling. At least, they danced around that topic several times, so he thought they had an understanding. She apparently didn't realize what kind of position this relationship was putting him in.

He had a morality clause in his contract as CEO, even though he owned forty-eight percent of the stock in the company. If the board decided there was any impropriety, they could band together and act against him. Of course, the clause specified a relationship between him and any employee, but the wife of an employee would have the same impact. It was still wrong.

His company was built on integrity and trust. His reputation was sound, and many of his business negotiations centered on that fact. He thought Elizabeth understood that.

"Unless the Lord builds the house, they labor in vain who build it." It was his mission statement. But he let lust and lies invade his house. And his conscience wouldn't let him rest.

He sent a quick message to his assistant.

"William, tell Yuri to wrap up this last negotiation and come home. He has earned a break. Tell him to spend time with his wife. Go on vacation. Take a month. A cruise around the Bahamas. My treat."

He wandered back to his bedroom, ready for sleep. But he could still feel the essence of her all around him. He smelled her perfume in the air, on his pillows. He recalled her dark eyes, candlelight dancing in them as they stared at each other over dinner. The softness of her fine silk dress in his fingers, the soft plop as it landed on the floor. Her beautiful toes rubbing against his leg.

He picked up his phone and sent another message, this time to his cleaning staff.

"I need a thorough scrubbing of my home. Detailed. Top to bottom. No later than seventy-two hours, please."

He sent one last message to William. *"Book a room for me at the hotel in One World. Tonight only."* He was leaving in the morning for his business trip. But he would not stay here tonight. When he returned, Elizabeth would be a distant memory.

———

"Yuri? Do you love me?" She looked at her husband with new eyes. Yuri was handsome, in a Middle Eastern way. Olive-colored skin, black wavy hair, and a slightly crooked nose from a fight with another boy when they were no more than ten. In her heels, she was taller than him. But that had never mattered, until now.

David had been gone for three weeks. A week longer than the

two he said he would be gone. Yuri had only been home for a few days, having delayed his return to swipe up another quick deal.

"I've been busy, Elizabeth. You know that. But you have everything you need here. What's wrong?"

"You haven't touched me since you've been home. You haven't even kissed me more than a peck on the cheek."

Their king-sized bed was large and left far too much room between them. How was she to tell him she needed him? That she craved his touch? Any touch. He had ignored her for so long now. When she noticed David staring at her from his own rooftop across the street, it was only natural that she would respond. Wasn't it? This whole thing wasn't her fault or David's fault. It was Yuri's fault. He started it by leaving her alone so much.

Tonight, she woke to find Yuri working at his laptop. What had happened to them? Why hadn't he even shown an ounce of interest in her since he came home? There might as well have been a brick wall between them in the middle of the sumptuous Cali-king. Or an ocean. That was it. There was an ocean between them in life and in love.

"Let me finish this last deal. My teams are working overseas while I am at home. Once we get it wrapped up, I will give them time off. It will take a few days, tops, then we will take a vacation, and I won't feel guilty about leaving them behind. Okay? I promise, somewhere warm. How about Hawaii? David has a property over there we can stay in, and I can check out the surrounding area while we are there."

"David, David, David! You are always doing something for him. What about me? I'm your wife, for Pete's sake." She paced back and forth, fuming.

A loud shriek filled the air. "Da-vid. Da-vid. Da-vid!"

Elizabeth paced by the bird cage, dropping the cover to silence the squawking macaw.

Yuri glared at the cage. "That thing needs to go."

"No. He keeps me company when you are gone. And besides, you bought him for me."

Yuri softened his stance and stopped her with his hand. He stood to kiss her cheek, his mustache tickling her soft skin. "I have a plan. One day we will retire and can go anywhere we want. But for now, I will be leaving again tomorrow. I just got a message about an urgent possibility."

"Then just go. Pete is the only man who really cares for me, anyway." She lifted her hand and scratched the spot where he had kissed her.

"Pete is a bird."

"That's better than being alone."

She left him to his work, choosing to sit on the terrace. The penthouse across the street was dark. There was no light, no movement, no one watching for her out the large sliding glass door. She sighed, realizing that she was alone again. Her stomach grew queasy.

Two days after Yuri left, she stared at her simple breakfast. One poached egg white, two pieces of melon, and an English muffin. All of it turned her stomach. The aromas mingled, creating a swirl of lava in her midsection, and suspicion rose in her mind as bile rose in her throat.

She ran to the bathroom, barely getting there before what little she had eaten spewed from her mouth. Sinking to the floor, she hung her head over the toilet bowl, fully aware of the significance of the act. It didn't matter how much money she had, or how fine a home she lived in. Whether her clothes were silk or polyester. If she shopped on Fifth Avenue or at a rural discount store. It could be solid gold. But a toilet was still a toilet.

She shoved her straight black hair behind her ears, lifting it with her hands and dropping it to flow down her back. Her stomach finally settled, and she stood. Finding a washcloth in the small linen closet, she washed her face and rinsed her mouth.

The mirror held her reflection, her eyes red and her skin pale. She realized she had missed a very important date. Now her body was showing signs. Tender breasts. Fatigue. She had slept past her normal eight a.m. wakeup time for the last few days. And of course, there was the undeniable lack of monthly flow. How had this happened? Hadn't they taken precautions? She thought back on all the times that she and David were together. There was that one time. The first time. The impulse that pulled them together like poles of a magnet. Oh, no.

"Oh, no. Oh, no." Pete squawked as she walked into the living room.

Elizabeth was starting to dislike that bird.

Her hand itched. The nervous habit was a definite tell to anyone who knew her. Her fingers scratched of their own accord, trying to calm the quirk. She rubbed them together to stop the motion.

What should she do now? She needed answers but was afraid to go out in public. It would not do for her to be recognized by anyone, but she had to know, so she wound a silk scarf around her head and slid dark shades over her eyes. The bright red, blue, and orange swirls of the scarf covered her hair and her fear, the oversized glasses hiding the pain in her face. She didn't even worry about makeup, which was very out of character. When she looked at her feet, she realized she still didn't have shoes on. Her designer stilettos mocked her from the shelves as she decided on flats. Reaching into the back of her closet, she found a raincoat she was going to donate to charity. It still had a stain on one sleeve where she had once spilled her coffee, and she regretted not having it cleaned. The stain was probably set in, now. Was her body stained, too? Her hands shook as she opened her door.

Taking her exclusive express elevator, she left her home and walked down the block to the corner pharmacy. The city noise grated on her nerves. Traffic, people, and street vendors all closed in on her as the tall buildings hovered around them. A garbage truck picked up a dumpster from behind a building, the sound reverberating through her as it dropped the heavy container back to the pavement. The odor of refuse joined forces with the smell of colognes, perfumes, and garlic on the patrons leaving a small pizza place. Clouds cast a gray pall, holding rain that threatened to escape its confines and wash the dirty streets. And her dirty heart.

She stopped in the middle of the sidewalk, letting others walk around her. What in the world was she doing? How did she get into this mess? Looking up, she realized she should have brought an umbrella. She was only half way and turned to go home.

She could order the test kits online. They would be sent in the normal smiling box and nobody would be the wiser. But no, she didn't want to wait that long. Not even until tomorrow. She had to know tonight.

She could use one of the courier services that catered to people needing immediate delivery on an item. But she didn't want anyone knowing what she was buying, and she didn't want them coming to her building. Gossip must be avoided at all cost.

Finally forcing her feet to move, she walked the remaining block and glanced around as she entered the store. A bell rang over her head, but nobody looked her way. She was just one of the ten or so people browsing the shelves of the small shop. Picking up a basket, she wished she had worn gloves. Dirt from the hundred people who used it before her was embedded into the plastic bottom. Did the store ever clean them?

She searched her purse for hand sanitizer and found the small bottle in the bottom. The strong odor of the alcohol in the cleansing substance made her head spin as she flipped open the cap. She quickly closed it and dropped it back into her purse, rubbing her hands together. The store spun before her, and she steadied herself against a shelf.

Once her vision stabilized, she decided to shop, picking up several items.

Makeup she would never use. Hers was specially blended for her by an exclusive company.

A pair of fuzzy socks. Cheap, but the hearts on them were cute. And they were infused with aloe. She might wear them as she relaxed at home.

A thermometer. The kind that scanned your forehead without touching.

Heartburn tablets. They might help ease her queasiness.

Two test kits. No, she added a third. To be sure. She stuffed them under everything else to make sure they were covered.

Stepping up to the cashier, her glasses slipped down her nose as she kept her head down. A man joined the line behind her and stood entirely too close, his overpowering cologne doing a poor job of covering the stale cigar smoke emanating from him. She gagged and swallowed. The clerk glanced at her, then looked at one of the boxes, reading the name as she scanned the tests.

"Oh, honey." The clerk patted her hand and leaned forward like she was telling a secret. "Don't worry. That pukiness will go away." Elizabeth placed her hand under her nose, then pulled it away when it smelled like the clerk's perfume. "These tests are really good. Accurate every time. I now have three beautiful children." The clerk smiled, her voice reverberating as others who were standing in line looked up. So much for the secret.

Elizabeth gulped again and shook her head, hoping the woman got the message. She would not stand there and talk with Ms. Chatty Check-Out Clerk. She never shopped at this store, but there may be others from her building who did. Paying for the items, she left as quickly as possible, the bag banging against the door as she hurried out. Bile rose again, and she hoped she hadn't been recognized.

A quick walk down the street brought her back to her building, where she marched through the garage and took the elevator to the top floor, bypassing the guard desk. Opening the door to her suite, she slipped inside, letting the soft hinges close it behind her. She flung the bag onto a table, then turned and locked her door. Nobody would walk in on her, but her nerves were on edge.

After removing her coat, glasses, and scarf, she picked up the bag and found the test kits. Her hands shook as she walked to the bathroom. The room of doom.

Taking a deep breath, she opened the first box and realized there were two test kits inside.

"How convenient. The clerk could have said something instead of letting me buy all those kits."

Following instructions, her hands continued to shake as she prepared the tests, dipped them as required, and set the timer on her phone. She lowered the toilet seat and sat down to wait.

Silence ticked by. Her phone dinged, but it was not the timer. Probably spam.

She walked into the kitchen, started to make a cup of coffee, then thought about the caffeine and stopped. Instead, she reached for a water glass and filled it from her filtered refrigerator. She drank the entire glass, then refilled it and drank that, too. She hadn't realized she was so thirsty.

The timer went off from the bathroom, its happy, melodic tones more irritating than soothing. She set her glass down on the kitchen island and made her way down the hall, feeling every step as if she was heading to an execution. She avoided looking at the tests while she turned off the timer. Looking around, she decided to sit. But she couldn't see the tests from there. So, she stood again, and finally forced herself to glance at them.

But the test kits told the truth. Both of them. She cried out to her empty apartment.

"Dear God. What am I going to do? Both men have abandoned me."

"Oh, no. Oh, no." The bird squawked her very thoughts.

She would have to hide the evidence. She couldn't let her maid see the test sticks or the packaging. She silently counted backwards to the first night they had been together. It was April Fool's Day. And oh, what a fool she had been.

Chapter Four

David walked into his office after being gone nearly a month, certain that was enough time for Elizabeth to forget him. Yuri had come home and taken his rightful place as her husband.

"Good morning, William."

"Good morning, sir. You look tanned and refreshed."

David laughed. "Three weeks in the Caymans will do that for you. What is on the agenda today?"

"I kept your schedule clear. Thought you might want some time to go through messages. I handled everything in your absence, but I know you like to be informed. And you have a full day tomorrow."

"Thank you, William. You are efficient, as always."

David spent the morning reviewing messages and reports from his various divisions. Yuri's report stood out, as always. Two new properties were acquired, and three sold. But wait. Wasn't he supposed to be home with his wife?

He frowned. His employee was an enigma. Why was he leaving his beautiful wife alone?

It was almost lunch time when he heard a commotion in the outer office. He looked up from his reports, ready to buzz William about the noise, when the assistant tapped on the doorframe, sticking his head inside the room.

"Come in." David's smile slipped. The look on William's face said something was wrong.

"Ms. Yassin is here. At my desk. I'm not sure how she got up here. She doesn't look happy."

"Where's Yuri?" David scrunched his eyebrows together.

"Japan, I believe." William scratched his jaw. David knew it was a nervous habit.

"Thank you, William. Send her . . ."

The door burst open. Elizabeth marched into the room, holding something in her hand. William bustled out after getting a quick nod of approval from David, leaving the door open. They had a corporate policy that no man would be left alone with a woman. It was designed to prevent any of them from being caught in a compromising situation. That included the CEO.

"Come on in, Elizabeth. But don't throw anything." He pointed to the leather chair in front of his desk and quickly moved a couple of objects to the credenza behind him. Far from her reach. He knew how to remain calm, even when faced with an angry woman. And he had seen her angry. It cost him eight thousand dollars to replace his glass door. He still wondered how it had shattered so completely.

She slapped something down on his desk, crossing her arms and tapping her foot. She was dressed in a designer skirt and blouse, her shoes from an upscale store. Probably on Fifth Avenue. Her jasmine perfume assaulted his nose, filling the air.

"What's this?" David was afraid to touch the small white plastic stick.

"This"—she pointed her manicured nail—"is ten weeks pregnant. That's what this is."

David stood and walked quickly to the door, closing it. This was one conversation he did not want even his assistant to overhear.

"And why is that important to me? Yuri is your husband." He went back to his desk and sat, folding his hands and linking his fingers, resting his elbows on the polished glass top. He would have to tread carefully.

"Yuri has been halfway around the world for months. And we both know this is not an immaculate conception. I've already been to the doctor to confirm it."

David unfolded his hands, picked up an ink pen, and tapped it on his desk. "What are you saying, Elizabeth? Did you have another lover?"

"No." She slumped into the chair, her arms hanging over the arms. "There was no one else, David."

The tension built between them. Neither of them was willing to state the obvious. To do so would have implications that neither wanted to admit. Especially David. He built his business on a standard of trust and integrity. If this got out . . .

"I'll bring Yuri home. He needs to be here to support you. For the birth of his child."

"Is that the way you want to spin this?" She challenged him with angry eyes as a tear slid down her cheek. "Yuri will know the baby is not his."

"Then do something about it, Elizabeth." He pulled two tissues out of a box that sat on his desk. He handed one to her and used the other to pick up the stick before giving it to her. He didn't want his fingerprints on it.

"What am I supposed to do? What do you want me to do?" Her words moaned the impossibility of the situation.

David watched her hands twist together. New York was a very pro-abortion state. Up to delivery, if he remembered correctly. But that thought turned his stomach. He didn't want to recognize the child as his—that would be admitting to the affair. No, the better option was to bring Yuri home to his wife.

"Would you like to visit the Orient? Yuri is in Japan. A vacation over there would be good for both of you. My treat. First Class." Out of sight, out of mind.

"No, David. I'm not going to Japan. I can barely keep my meals down. I can't imagine spending hours over the ocean, stuck in a seat between smelly passengers. Even if it is First Class. And I would still have nothing to do while he is hanging out with snobs."

"Snobs? That's a rather arrogant statement." David raised an eyebrow.

"You know what I mean, David. The answer is no. I am not going anywhere." She fisted her hand, elbow on the arm of the chair, and rested her cheek against it.

"Fine. I will bring Yuri to you."

He buzzed William, who entered quickly. "Ms. Yassin is leaving, now. And please call maintenance for a portable air filter."

Her lovely perfume had become an annoyance.

———

"William, we need to bring Yuri home. He can work from here and delegate the site visits to others."

The assistant escorted Elizabeth to the elevator and made sure it reached the bottom before returning to David's office.

"I will reach out to him and make the arrangements today. And maintenance will bring a filter up within the hour. Is everything all right with Ms. Yassin?"

"She's fine. Just misses her husband."

David dismissed his assistant and slumped back into his chair. He swiveled once and stood up. Looked through the window at the city that he fought and scrapped over for years, finally making his way. He could see over the horizon from here. Most people couldn't see beyond the next block.

His father always told him that life was a series of choices. Each choice would affect the future choices that would be placed in front of him. Mountains were made to be climbed. Valleys were made to be traversed. Rivers made to be crossed. But people. People were made to be, what? Loved? Respected? Served? Used?

His first wife was his first love. Abigail was the girl next door, an all-American, loved apple pie and baseball, went to church every Sunday kind of girl. Born and raised in the heartland of Iowa, they attended Iowa State together and married the day after graduation. She even helped him on some of his first real estate transactions. But when he went away to business school, she stayed home. And it wasn't long before the distractions of life came between them and the marriage fell apart. The last he heard, she'd married a farmer, and they had four kids. He shook his head at the memories.

Allison was his second wife and much more refined. But she was a social climber. They met in business school, at a party hosted by one of the ambitious elites, and stayed together until he began travelling to build his business. It didn't take her long to find a billionaire on Wall Street. He remembered coming home from a trip to England to an empty apartment and empty bank account. Fortunately, he had multiple personal accounts and wasn't as broke as she thought he was.

Since then, he focused on becoming one of the richest men in the United States. He moved in and out of the highest echelons of society. Charity events and political fundraisers were on his calendar every month. His closet hosted multiple tuxedos that were tailor-made of the finest silks and wools. People begged to work with him. Schools now used case studies of his business model in their curriculum, and interns were eager to ride his coattails.

Women flocked to him, and yes, he had entertained plenty. A temporary dalliance was fine, as long as there wasn't a husband in the way. The women always understood it was temporary. The relationships were brief and the partings mutual. No emotion, no harm. Even though he knew, in the back of his mind, that it wasn't quite right.

But now. Now, he was faced with the consequence of another dalliance. And this consequence was permanent.

A baby. A beating heart. A piece of his DNA.

He pounded his fist against the fortified window. What if the baby looked like him? Had his blue eyes? His Caucasian coloring?

Elizabeth and Yuri both have brown eyes and olive skin.

He didn't believe in abortion. That was one thing he could not abide. Life was life, no matter how you looked at it. But he couldn't claim the baby as his, either. It would destroy everything he had worked for. Everything he planned. And the livelihoods of the hundreds of people who worked for him here in the tower, not to mention those who worked in his diversified divisions, would be crushed. If his business failed because of this mistake, thousands of people would suffer.

He still owned controlling interest in the company. His board could not fire him, could they? He would have to check with Nathan.

His attorney had been his friend since college. David went on to get his MBA, while Nathan went to law school. But they remained friends and reconnected after receiving their respective degrees. Nathan might be upset at first, but he would understand. Wouldn't he?

Was the lawyer farsighted enough to see beyond David's involvement with Elizabeth? Like his view from the towering spire? Or was he as nearsighted as the people on the street below?

No. He wouldn't tell Nathan right away. He would stick with the plan to bring Yuri home. Let Elizabeth take care of the situation.

Chapter Five

Elizabeth sat at her dressing table, studying a wrinkle she found on her face before glancing up. Was that a gray hair? She moved her hand from her face to the top of her head. This would never do. She would have to contact her hairdresser.

The stress must be getting to her. Yuri would be home later this afternoon. She would need to be on her best game, welcome him with open arms, seduce him with love, remind him of the passion they shared when first married. They could rekindle that again. They would have to.

David had not acknowledged anything. She didn't know why that surprised her. Did she expect him to pledge his undying love? Ask her to divorce her husband and marry him? At least set up a trust fund for the baby? But, no. He had not offered anything. Just told her to go home to her husband and make him think the baby was his.

Did he really think no one would count the months?

She thought of the small pill sitting in her medicine cabinet. The doctor prescribed the mifepristone when he confirmed her pregnancy. New York allowed abortion all the way up to delivery. But that thought turned her stomach, and she was already nearing the end of her tenth week. That was the cutoff for use of the pill.

Thinking quickly, she ran to her bathroom and flushed the pill down the toilet. She also found a paper bag and stuffed the box inside, burying the whole thing deep in her trash can. She didn't want Yuri, or her maid, to find it.

The front door opened with a thud and a couple of muttered oaths as she covered the evidence. Yuri. She rinsed her hands then rushed to meet her husband.

"Sweetheart! You're home. I have missed you so much." She kissed him briefly before helping him with his coat, hanging it in the closet of their small entryway, and taking his hand, leading him to their sofa.

"You look tired. Was it a long trip? Let me get you something to drink." She started toward their wet bar. She had looked up the flight time from Japan to New York. Nonstop was twelve hours. It would have been an excruciating flight.

"I don't want anything to drink, Elizabeth." He yanked away from her, plopping into a cushioned chair instead of the sofa. He rubbed his hand over his face, peering at her from between his fingers.

"I was this close to completing that last deal. This close." He held his fingers up, pinching his thumb and forefinger together. "What does David do? He reassigns the deal and orders me to come home. Orders me. If I did something to upset him, he didn't say. Just said, 'Come home to your wife.'"

Elizabeth stopped in front of the bar. He stood and stalked toward her, leaning close to invade her space. There was already a distinct odor of alcohol on his breath. His lips curled in a feral smile.

"So, wife, what is going on?" His look bore through Elizabeth, his finger pointed in her face. "What have you done that is so important I had to be pulled out of negotiations on a multimillion-dollar deal to rush home to you?" Fire shot from his dark brown eyes, the golden glints in his irises like sparks lighting up a night sky.

"Me? What makes you think I did anything?" What did he know? Elizabeth scratched her hands together. She wanted to bite the accusing finger.

"Tell me, Elizabeth. Tell me." His face was red with rage.

She had to diffuse this situation quickly. Setting the glass and decanter she was holding on the bar, she took his hand, lacing her fingers between his and pushing a strand of his rich black hair off his forehead with the other. She rested her body against his and whispered in his ear.

"I've missed you, Yuri. You must know that." She squeezed his hand to punctuate the statement.

"That's it? You missed me? You went to my boss and asked him to bring me home because you missed me? You interfered in my job." He stepped back and shook his hand free. "You have made me a laughingstock, Elizabeth. The deal was reassigned to a rookie. A rookie who had no experience with such large deals."

He paced away, running his fingers through the ebony strands she had just touched.

"I love you, Yuri. I need you." She held her stomach, unable to stop the queasiness that was building. Unfortunately, he noticed the move, and his eyes narrowed.

"Are you sick? Is that it?" His look turned from anger to concern.

If he thought she was sick he would show more sympathy. But she wouldn't accomplish her goal that way, either. "No, not sick." She cast her eyes downward, the words coming out weak. She couldn't tell him yet. He would know he was not the father.

"Then what, Elizabeth? Stop playing games with me." He spun, grabbing his suitcase. "I think I'll go to a hotel for the night. I am too angry to even look at you."

"Please don't. I'll make it up to you. I promise. Just give me one night." She reached for him, knowing she was groveling, but she didn't know what else to do. He walked out anyway, without another word.

The door shut behind him with a click, but the sound reverberated in her heart like a cannon shot. Giving in, she picked up the decanter and threw it onto her marble floor, the shattered pieces and amber liquid scattering across the pale gray-and-white tile. Standing alone in the middle of the room, she shook her head. This was becoming a pattern. She glanced down at the coffee table in front of her sofa and cringed at the magazine laying there. Piercing blue eyes mocked her from the cover.

Stepping around the glass and out onto the terrace, she raised her eyes to the building next door. David stood on his own terrace, hands on his hips, looking out over the city. Had he heard them arguing? She backed next to the wall to keep from being seen. Stars twinkled overhead. It should be a beautiful night. But inside her heart, all her lights had gone out.

———

David called Yuri into his office the following Monday.

"How was your reunion with your wife? I imagine you spent most of the time indoors." David winked at his vice president of foreign acquisitions.

"That is none of your business. But if you must know, I'm staying at a hotel."

David frowned. "What happened?"

Yuri sighed. "It's like we don't know each other anymore. And I don't appreciate you letting her interfere with my job." He stood and paced.

"You've been working too hard lately. She simply pointed that out to me. I've been asking too much of you."

Yuri continued to walk back and forth, his stride quick and sharp. His face grew red from fuming.

"She just wants to spend time with you." David pleaded with Yuri. Normally, he would never be involved in his employees' personal lives, but this was a different situation.

"How would you know that?" Yuri spun, his finger pointed at David.

David froze at the question and accusing finger. But only for a moment. He crossed his arms and stared down his friend, holding his gaze. It was the kind of look his father gave him as a teenager. It said he was the boss. Period.

"Elizabeth is my wife. And our marriage is none of your concern." Yuri was still angry, but his tone was softer.

"Our annual corporate gala is in two weeks. You need to be there, with Elizabeth on your arm." David stood, leading Yuri to the sofa on the other side of the room.

"Why? I'm thinking of divorcing her. She has turned into a shrew." Yuri plopped down into the soft leather cushion, slouching like a disgruntled teenager.

"Yuri, our company has a certain reputation to maintain. Trust. Integrity. Family. Our customers want to see that in action."

"And what about you?" Yuri turned on David and sneered. "Where is your wife? Oh. That's right. Abby left you. Or was it Allison?"

"We were still in college. Too young." David needed to nip this in the bud. Not many people had the nerve to speak to him like that. Especially not his employees. But it would do no good to feed Yuri's anger. He wondered what Elizabeth told him.

"You've earned the time off. According to HR, you have nearly three months of vacation time racked up, just waiting to be taken. Go home to your wife. Spend time getting to know each other again. Take her shopping for a new dress for the gala. You had romance with her once. Do things to rekindle that again."

Yuri stood. "I don't know why it is so important to you that I spend time with my wife. Unless you know something you're not telling me?" He glared, but David wouldn't take the bait. Yuri huffed. "Have it your way. I will take two weeks off. Beyond that, I make no promises."

David watched as Yuri left his office and felt the tension leave with his vice president. But the problem still remained.

Chapter Six

The Independence Day gala was held at the observatory on the hundred and second floor, soaring a quarter mile above the streets below. Lights twinkled throughout the ballroom like red, white, and blue fairies. Round tables covered in white jacquard tablecloths held short centerpieces of blue delphiniums, white roses, and red candles. They were staged around the edges of the room, providing guests with a heavenly view of the rivers and cities below, and the fireworks that would be shot high into the air over the harbor. One end was reserved for a stage, its backdrop a stunning view of the city behind them, where a string quartet played softly. They would give way after dinner to a lively dance band. The black granite floor was polished to a high sheen, providing a perfect place for dancing the night away.

David circled the room, welcoming employees and honored guests. He always included some of his more influential clients to this event as a thank you for their business. A happy customer would tell others, and a good recommendation from a client was one of the best advertisements.

Movement at the door caught his eye. Yuri and Elizabeth entered together. David nearly wiped his forehead in relief, but his eyes lit up at the dress she wore. Red silk draped and clung to her, swaying with her hips as she walked. The split up her thigh stopped just short of scandalous, but not much. Her mere presence had David recalling every inch of her beautiful body as she gave herself to him. Checking his gaze, he lowered his eyes as his heart began to beat faster. He could not show interest.

They made their way to the bar. David watched from across the room as the bartender poured a drink for each of them. But he noticed that Elizabeth only pretended to drink hers before setting the glass down. When the bartender handed her a glass of water with lemon, he acted like he was going to say something, but she shook her head. And, like a good bartender, he lowered his head to mind his own business.

"Great party, David. You throw a good one, as always." Antoni Yusavi, a mentor for many years and one of his primary board members, slapped his shoulder.

"Thanks, Antoni. I would like to take the credit, but my assistant, William, worked with the event planner here to put everything together. I didn't have to lift a finger."

"It's called management, David. And you do it well." The man pointed toward the bar. "Is that Yuri over there? Is he finally home from his world travels?"

The man's gaze lingered on Elizabeth, and David wondered why. Not that he couldn't enjoy God's beautiful creation, but David couldn't sort out the look on his face. It was a cross between admiring her figure and that of a loving father. Strange.

Black hair with streaks of gray and olive skin spoke of Antoni's heritage. He almost looked a bit like Elizabeth. But that couldn't be. Antoni was from New York. Elizabeth moved with her husband from Turkey when Yuri was first hired by David. They couldn't possibly be related.

"Yes, he is home for a well-deserved vacation. I think I've convinced him to take some extended time. If he wants to work, he can do it here from the office and parse out those long trips to his staff."

"Not to mention finally getting time with his beautiful wife."

The board member nodded his head, a gleam in his eye, before walking over to the pair to say hello. David shook his head. Antoni was a family man but he would still admire a beautiful woman. Made him wonder, sometimes.

An hour later, Elizabeth caught up to him as he stood on the sidelines, leaning against a wall. She sidled up to him, her dress and perfume taunting him.

"Dance with me?"

"In front of everyone? I hardly thing that's wise, Elizabeth." He looked around to make sure they hadn't been overheard.

"It's not working." Her lips turned down in a pout.

"What's not working?" David was confused.

"Yuri. Being home. He stays up late every night and gets up early in the morning. He says he is working on Greenwich Mean Time, whatever that means. At any rate, I never see him.

"He has been home for almost two weeks. Are you telling me you haven't been able to work your magic on him?" David kept his eyes on the room as he spoke to her, his voice low.

"I think he's suspicious. Either that, or he's having his own affair. I hear him on the phone when he thinks I'm not listening. They aren't his normal business calls. He talks about stock prices and shares. I don't know. He could just be talking to his financial advisor. But when he sees me nearby, he changes the subject like he's talking to an old friend. And he goes out to dinner, but doesn't take me. He says he is meeting friends. At night, he waits until he thinks I'm asleep before he comes into the bedroom."

David considered her words. Yuri was a trusted employee. A man of his word. His marriage to Elizabeth had seemed to be solid. Was there was something else going on? Whatever it was, they were running out of time. Elizabeth's lovely figure would soon turn round.

"You must make it work tonight. Get him happily drunk. Do what you do best." David quirked his eyebrow at her.

"You would know what that is, wouldn't you?"

"Yuri is looking this way. Go to him." He lifted his hand, holding a glass of his favorite drink, and pointed that direction.

She nodded and strutted away, reminding him from behind of what she does best.

———

Fireworks lit up the sky over New York Harbor. Bright explosions of red, white, and blue celebrated the birthday of America. Of freedom. Party attendees oohed and aahed as they moved toward the windows to watch the display. Music played from speakers around the room, piping in the feed from the festivities outside. The display was perfectly timed, as always.

The view from a hundred floors up was unlike any other. It was like being right there in the sky, floating in the air with the bursting, twinkling colors surrounding them. Huge, bright shapes. Stars, hearts, flowers. Sunbursts that looked like puffy dandelion heads. Rainbows in a spectrum to rival God's. Sparks flashed, and some floated below them as they made their way toward the water before burning out. Watching it from this perspective was different than the view from the ground. It was exhilarating. Powerful.

Kingston Holdings, Incorporated was one of the primary sponsors of the event. It took an entire year to plan. In fact, after only one night off, the management company would begin working with their suppliers and experts from the other side of the world on next year's theme. Sometimes they used show tunes. One year it was classic rock. But usually it was patriotic. Tonight, it was John Philips Sousa.

He scanned the room and found two of his board members, heads down in earnest discussion. They glanced at him once, then turned their backs, completely ignoring him and the fireworks. David strolled across the room to join them.

"Evening, gentlemen."

"Oh. David. Hello." James and Grayson were valuable investors and stockholders, each heading up different divisions. James oversaw the transportation division, and Grayson oversaw energy.

"Enjoying the festivities?" Fireworks shot into the sky, brightening their faces in flashes of color, and the rousing patriotic music threatened to drown out their conversation.

"Wonderful party, David. As always." The two men looked at each other.

"You're missing the show out there. Is there something important I should know about?" He didn't know what was going on, but he had the feeling that they were up to something.

"Not at all." The two men glanced at each other again. "Just looking at another investment outside of Kingston. If we think it is a good fit, we'll loop you in."

"Well, keep me informed. And enjoy the night."

David walked away, an uneasy feeling in his stomach. He always listened to those gut reactions. Well. Almost always. At any rate, he would talk to William about keeping a closer watch on them. He wished he could say he trusted them completely, but then, this was New York. There was always somebody with ulterior motives.

The senator approached, a glass of swirling amber liquid in his hand. He was another board member and significant investor. And another one to watch. His wife was on his arm, a ravishing redhead with not a wrinkle in sight. But they had been married for almost thirty years and were a power couple. A stripe of gray was slicked back in his hair that was brown with golden highlights. Only his hairdresser knew what was real and what wasn't.

"Great gala, David."

"Thank you, Senator. I'm glad you could join us this year."

"Well, you know me. I'm always campaigning for something. But I just came over to say hello." He laid his hand on David's shoulder.

David laughed. "Senator, you never just say hello. What can I do for you?"

The senator pulled David away from James and Grayson. He had an idea for a new partnership with investors from Hong Kong.

David wasn't interested in that kind of deal, but he would listen. Meanwhile, he saw James and Grayson watching them from across the room, smug smiles on their faces. Yes. Something was definitely going on. Elizabeth's comments about Yuri's phone calls and dinners added to his unease.

Nathan strolled by with a gorgeous blonde on his arm. "Hello David. You remember my wife, Gloria?" She was dressed very conservatively in a midnight blue dress that sparkled as she moved. A few wrinkles lined her blue eyes, and she wore them with grace. Her beauty was genuine. No Botox for her.

"Nathan. You made it. Good to see you again, Gloria." He reached out to shake his attorney's hand.

"We've actually been here for a bit. You seem to have been occupied elsewhere." Nathan waved his hand to indicate the room. "No date, tonight?"

"No. You know I like to fly solo at these things. I need to make sure all my guests have a good time. Besides, there isn't anyone special at the moment."

Nathan's eyes examined the room, stopping on Elizabeth. He narrowed his eyes. "Right. We need to find you a woman. Get you happily married." He looked at his wife. "What do you say, Gloria? Do you know anyone at church who would be a good fit for David?"

David groaned. "Been there, done that. And it didn't work. I'm perfectly fine like I am. But I appreciate your concern." He winked at Gloria, who shook her head, then he pulled Nathan aside and lowered his voice.

"Do me a favor, please. I need financials for all my board members. Something is up."

"What do you suspect?"

"Not sure yet. Call it a gut feeling." The one time David had not trusted his gut, it got him into trouble. This time, he would not ignore the warning.

"Well, I trust your gut. Give me a couple of days after we get back in the office." Nathan turned back to his wife and continued their stroll around the room.

David strolled the other direction, his eyes on Elizabeth, who was plying Yuri with drinks. He hoped she was successful tonight. Otherwise, he didn't know what he would do.

———

Elizabeth woke the next morning and looked over at her husband. She succeeded in getting him home, but little else because he was too drunk. She closed the space between them and wrapped herself around him. Let him think what he would. She kissed his strong jaw, enjoying the feel of his luscious black hair through her fingers and the scruff that had grown on his face overnight.

"Good morning, lover."

"Ugh. Good morning, I think." He rubbed his eyes with the palms of his hands. "Fireworks are going off in my brain."

"Headache?" She made the word drip with sweetness.

"Yeah. It was a very fuzzy night. I'm not used to drinking that much."

"Well, I thought it was a wonderful night. A dazzling display over the harbor, and an even more dazzling night at home." She stretched like a cat, making her point.

"I'm glad you're pleased. I don't remember a moment of it."

"Let me get you something for that hangover." She left the bed, snatching her satin robe from the end of the bed and draping it around herself before heading to the medicine cabinet in their ensuite bathroom. Returning with two pain relievers, she handed them to him, then made a second trip for a glass of water. He scooted up against the pillows and leaned his head against the plush headboard.

"What shall we do today, husband?" She winked and crawled back into bed with him.

"Nothing. I'm going to check messages. Work never stops, you know."

She laid her hand on his arm. "Work can stop for one day. Take me shopping. I feel like a new dress. I want to make your eyes pop out of your head."

"You go shopping. You don't need my opinion. And you just wore a new dress last night. Why do you need another one?" He reached for his nightstand to pick up his phone. She pulled it from his hand and stuffed it under her pillow, her hand returning to his chest.

"Spend the day with me."

"Tomorrow. I promise." He reached around her to find the phone, snagging it back and rolling away. He immediately began checking his messages.

She pursed her lips into a frown. Rising from the bed, she went to the kitchen, needing coffee. She didn't know how she was going to accomplish what David expected of her. Her husband had become impossible, in all aspects.

"Good morning." Pete gave his normal greeting.

She greeted the bird after filling her coffee cup with her special blend. It turned her stomach, the bile rising, but she was able to push it down. It would not do for Yuri to see her vomit. She dumped the coffee into the sink and got a glass of water.

The bird whistled and sang her off key show song. What was she going to do?

Clouds obscured the sun, and her heart. She had not accomplished her mission last night. Although, hopefully his memory was fuzzy enough he wouldn't know the difference.

"I've got to leave town, Elizabeth. There is a deal in Jordan that I don't dare give to anyone else to manage. I just got the message this morning." Yuri walked into the room and poured himself a cup of her special blend.

"You promised to take me shopping."

"No. I told you to go shopping. You don't need me."

"Why Jordan? Why would David do business there?"

"The location is in Amman, the capital. It's not just a real estate deal. It's an important business deal. But I can't say more than that. I'll be working with the government there." He pointed his gaze at her. "You forget, I was born in the Middle East. I have the cultural and lingual knowledge to make this deal successful."

"You were born in Turkey."

"Which is where I met David when he was on a business trip, and why we came to America. Look. I'm sorry. I know I was supposed to be home for a while. But I'm the best person to do this. You know that."

"I was born in Israel. I loathe those people. You can't do this to me." She picked at her fingernails. It was time to go back to the salon.

He took her hands in his, and she wanted to pull away. She needed crackers, but that might make him suspicious. He could not go to Jordan. Not now.

She was near the end of her third month. Soon she would be in her second trimester and begin showing. Would he come back to her? She didn't know why, but she had an overwhelming fear that this trip would go badly. Her hand automatically moved to her stomach. A flutter danced there, although she knew it was far too early for that.

Yuri kissed her softly. How long had it been? It was a chaste kiss but she determined that was better than nothing. Would it be their last?

"Jordan and Turkey have a good relationship. I will be completely safe." He stepped away. "I'll be working all day here to prep for the visit, and I'll sleep in the other bedroom tonight. I leave very early in the morning and don't want to disturb you. I'll be back in a few weeks. I promise."

"I'll be back. I'll be back."

"Shut up, bird." Yuri snapped.

"Shut up, bird. Shut up, bird."

Elizabeth wanted to cry and throw something. But her maid had already commented on the other messes she had to clean up, and Elizabeth didn't want the woman to quit. So, she went into their bedroom and stuffed her face into her pillow, her scream quietly absorbed by the fluffy down feathers.

Chapter Seven

David opened his white paneled door. He had received notice on his phone that the elevator was on its way up. But he wasn't expecting anyone, and all deliveries were made to the guard station on the first floor. Whoever it was must have bypassed the desk. He would call his security company tomorrow and add cameras to the elevator.

He heard the ding and watched as the doors opened. Elizabeth stood there, her mouth turned down, looking forlorn but still beautiful. Did the woman not understand the meaning of *no*?

"What are you doing here?"

"It's Friday night. Yuri is gone again, doing your business. And I'm lonely."

Her plea seemed genuine. Moreover, he had to admit that he had sent Yuri to Jordan. David sighed, one hand on the doorknob and the other on his hip. He looked up at the ceiling, denial spinning through his head. He should tell her to go home. This could lead to nothing good. But his body took over, training his thoughts in another direction. He fixed his gaze on her face, her eyes hopeful, and stepped back into his penthouse, sweeping his free hand inward.

"Come on in."

Elizabeth entered the living area. She was dressed simply in a sleeveless top that flowed around her waist, and high-end jeans. But she still had on her signature heels. The woman never shopped at a discount store and never went anywhere without her five-inch stilettos. She laid her jacket over the back of his designer sofa and kicked off her shoes.

"Make yourself at home, Elizabeth." It was meant to be a facetious statement, but she took it literally as she plopped onto the couch to rub her feet. "I was just about to eat dinner, but I have enough for two. My cook always makes extras on the weekends."

"I'm not hungry, David." The look in her eye said something different.

"Sit down with me and have some wine, then, while I eat. Because I am hungry." But he was not that kind of hungry. Not tonight. Not with her.

"No wine, David. Water is fine. Have you forgotten already?"

She raised her eyebrows at him as a reminder. No. He had not forgotten. But he did put it way back in the recesses of his mind.

Her dark brown eyes followed him as he ate his grilled tilapia filet. She turned the stem of her glass back and forth in her hand, taking an occasional sip. The silence lengthened between them. He knew he was ignoring her, but he did not want to raise the questions he feared she would ask. So, he waited for her to speak first.

"What are we going to do, David?"

And there it was. He eyeballed her slim figure. Was she in her second trimester yet?

"Your husband has been home, hasn't he? I'm assuming he knows he is going to be a father." He took another bite, wanting to appear nonchalant. But inside, his nerves were quivering.

"No. I haven't told him. I need to wait a little longer."

"Longer? By my calculation, you don't have much time. In fact, I'd say you have already run out of time. He was home for two weeks. What did you do during that time?"

"By my calculation, if I tell him now, he will know the baby isn't his." Elizabeth huffed and went back to the sofa, picking up a pillow and holding it over her stomach as she sat.

David pushed his plate aside and stood. What did she want from him? He walked to the terrace and slid the door open, stepping out into the twilight sky. Summer was progressing, and the air was warmer now. But there was a chill in his heart.

He felt rather than heard her as she stepped up behind him and laid her hand on his arm, her feet still bare. She set her glass on a nearby table and faced him. Her jasmine perfume swirled around them.

"There is nothing to hold us back tonight. Yuri is in Jordan. We are here. And I'm already pregnant, so there is no danger of that happening." She paused for a brief moment and moved closer. "I'm afraid. Hold me tonight. Please."

David glanced across the street at the empty terrace, almost willing Yuri to step out of those sliding doors. To challenge him for the honor of his wife. But that didn't happen. The nature of the business in Jordan meant he had to have his best men. His best man. And Yuri was the man for that job.

"What are you afraid of? Women have been giving birth since God made Adam and Eve." He shook his head. He'd heard that pregnancy made women moody.

"It's not that. I can't explain it. It's like I know something is going to happen. Something bad. But I don't know what it is, and there's nothing I can do to stop it."

"You're imagining things, Elizabeth. Your hormones are working overtime." He took a step back.

"Please?" A tear tracked down her cheek, and she closed that step again.

He took a long breath and wrapped his arms around her, leaning his chin on her head and inhaling her jasmine perfume. Would he regret this night? Probably. He already had too many regrets.

"Let's go inside."

———

David's phone rang at two in the morning. He almost ignored it, but then he recognized the ring he assigned to Jonas, the project lead on the Jordan team. The name on the screen confirmed the caller. It was nine a.m. in Jordan. What was going on there? He pushed Elizabeth aside, rolled away from her, and picked up the phone.

"David, here."

He could barely understand the caller for the panic in his voice, but he heard the last word. ". . . bombing."

Jumping from the bed, he grabbed his pants from the floor, and moved into the living room, closing the bedroom door behind him.

"Jonas. Slow down. I can't understand you. Take a breath, and count to five." Sirens echoed in the background, along with the sounds of people running and shouting. Where was he calling from? David inwardly counted to five to slow Jonas down, along with his own breathing. "Okay now. What do you mean, bombing? Is everyone okay?"

"It was a car bomb, David. The team was walking down the street from the hotel to the office when the car blew up. Right in front of us. We were barely a block away when it happened." The sirens were suddenly muted. Jonas must have stepped inside a building.

"Can you get everyone to the embassy?"

"It's too late. Three people are in the hospital. And three people are dead. Yuri is dead."

David sat down on the sofa. He heard his bedroom door open and glanced up, seeing Elizabeth walk out with his shirt wrapped around her, and refocused on the call.

"Are you injured?"

"No. I was farther back, behind the team, and the blast somehow missed me." His voice shook. "I don't know how this happened."

"Where are you now?"

David heard the man draw in a deep breath. His adrenaline must be running high right now. He could imagine Jonas standing up straighter as he pulled himself together. Don't let emotion control the situation.

"I'm at the hospital. I've already given a brief police statement, and I will probably have to make another one, more detailed. Then I'll find out where the team members that are still alive will be transferred to get them out of Jordan. We can't send them to Israel, even though that is closer and they have a great trauma center there. It will probably be Germany instead. I'll need to arrange for evacs. I'll also head to the coroner's office after I leave here to follow up on those who died." He took another long breath. "And I'll follow up with the client." He was silent for a moment. "I'll send all the details as quickly as possible."

"Thanks, Jonas. Don't worry about the client. We will follow up from here. I'll also get our crisis team deployed from this end to help you. One more question. Do you think we were targeted, or was it aimed at someone else?" The visit involved the Jordanian government, and was sensitive in nature. But who would want to take out his team?

"It was not quite eight a.m, a little over an hour ago. The street was crowded with people going to work, so it is hard to say. Several other people were injured, as well."

David ran a hand over his face. Elizabeth poured a strong drink and handed it to him. She watched him as he listened to Jonas and must have seen his stress. He pushed the drink away. He had to keep a clear head. She returned with water.

"Has the bombing hit the news, yet?" He picked up a remote and touched a button to reveal a television hidden inside the wall. But he looked up at Elizabeth again, seeing her stare, and realized she was listening closely, so he didn't turn it on. He turned away from her and cupped his hand over the phone.

"I don't have a TV nearby, so I couldn't say. But reporters are swarming the place, so I'm sure it will air soon, if it hasn't already."

David glanced back over his shoulder. Elizabeth now stood

across the room, scanning her phone. Horror was splashed across her face. So the news was out. Hopefully they hadn't listed any names yet, but foreign media didn't always follow the same rules about holding information until next of kin were notified.

"Thank you for the update, Jonas. Send me the details in an email. I will need to contact Nathan and prepare to make a statement in the morning."

"Do you want me to call Elizabeth?" The sounds of sirens grew louder then dimmed. A door must have opened and closed.

"No." David watched her from across the room. "I will take care of that. I think that is an in-person conversation. But I will call Nathan and ask him to inform the families of the other victims."

He ended the call and walked over to Elizabeth, gently took the phone from her hand and glanced at the screen, then set it face down on the dining table. Taking both her hands in his, he led her back to the sofa.

"I know what you are going to say." She looked blandly at their joined hands. A tear rolled down her cheek.

"I'm sorry, Elizabeth. Yuri was caught in the blast. He's dead."

"My husband is dead." It was a quiet statement. Like she had forgotten all about their relationship. Their affair. Why she was in his apartment tonight.

"And I am here. With you."

No, she hadn't forgotten. Her face held the calm before the storm that he knew would come. He hoped his next words offered comfort.

"I'll take care of everything, Elizabeth. I'll make sure you have enough money to last the rest of your life."

She stood and paced back and forth, scrubbing her hands over her head until her glorious mane of hair was wild mess. Then she swiveled and speared him with her eyes.

"You think this is about money? Is that all you think about? I just lost my husband!" She beat her fists on his chest, her dark brown orbs flashing with flecks of fire while tears streamed down her beautiful face.

He stared at her for several seconds before responding, letting her beat her frustration out on him. What could he say to comfort her? Was she worried because Yuri was dead? After the events of the past few weeks, he didn't think that was the case. They were on the verge of divorce, according to Yuri. It must be about money. It had to be.

"I'm sorry. That was crass of me." Women always wanted apologies. He didn't know what else to say.

"How dare you? How dare you take the life of that beautiful man? The man who was so devoted to you that he didn't even know what was going on under his own nose." She went to the bar and picked up a decanter.

"Please don't throw it." He hadn't killed her husband. But it wouldn't do any good to argue with her right now.

She stared at him until the words registered. Then she set the decanter back on the bar.

He tried to read her expression as she wiped her cheeks, pulling herself together. She marched with a different focus toward the bedroom, picking up her clothes along the way. Two minutes later she came out of the room, fully dressed. But her face was now made of stone, devoid of any emotion at all.

"Elizabeth. I'm sorry. Again. But I think we are both in shock. Let's take a moment and discuss this rationally." He stood and held out his arms.

"Rationally? I'll show you rationally." She picked up the decanter again and whirled this time, aiming for the television. Fortunately, he anticipated the action and caught the cut crystal container before it could fly across the room. She stepped toward him, mere inches from his face. He could see the anger swirling as her face reddened and her eyes glared.

"I will need to make funeral arrangements. I'll send the name of the mortuary to Nathan." She spit her final words through clenched teeth and left through the same paneled door he opened to her last night, letting it close on its own. Her jasmine perfume lingered behind.

He sat back down on the sofa, the soft leather doing nothing to calm his nerves. But he was CEO of a mega conglomerate. He did not allow his emotions to control him. Turning on his television, he scrolled through the channels, looking for news of the car bomb. The story was on every major news outlet, the AP and Reuters feeds providing more speculation than fact. Flipping to the streaming channels, he found the same, the reports all carbon copies of each other.

He had a mess on his hands. He hadn't killed her husband, and he hoped she would calm down enough to realize that. Other members of the team died as well. More were injured. A rogue faction was taking credit for the act of aggression, according to the petite reporter who smiled to the camera, head covered in a black silk scarf, while she relayed the latest details. His team just happened to be caught in the middle.

He turned his head and stared at the paneled door that closed behind Elizabeth. Would she talk to the media? And if so, what would she say? Between the affair, the pregnancy, and now a dead husband, she could insinuate enough to bring him down.

———

Elizabeth was in shock. She wasn't even thirty years old, and already a widow. She shivered as she rode the elevator down to the first level, lack of sleep combined with the news overcoming her body with stress. Her adrenaline was fading fast.

The street was still at this hour of the morning, traffic seeming to understand her grief. She looked both ways before stepping onto the sidewalk, suddenly fearful of what may lurk in the shadows. Crossing quickly to her building, she took her own elevator to her suite, swiped her key over the lock of her door, and entered her quiet apartment. Pete shuffled in his cage, the cover in place, as she slumped down onto her sofa. She was tempted to zip back the cover, just to hear his greeting.

"Good morning, Pete." She whispered the words, not wanting to disturb him.

Staring into the darkness, she kicked her shoes off and pulled her knees to her chest, hugging herself, crossing her ankles, and letting her feet rest on the soft cushion. Minutes ticked by, the silence threatening to consume her. Numbness set in, and she pulled a blanket from the back of her designer sofa, wrapped it around her shoulders, and let her tears and thoughts flow.

Widow.

The word was meant for somebody twice her age. Someone who was more prepared for the brevity of life, their gray hairs having been earned by surviving trials. Not by being a victim to them.

Would she wear black for a year? She didn't want to. She wanted to live. She had too much of life ahead of her. Sadness overshadowed her thoughts. Her life had taken a sudden detour.

Car bomb.

They moved to America for freedom and safety. He was caught in the Middle East violence, anyway. Was there any place in the world that was truly safe? Why move here, away from her family, if he was still going to die? Was he killed instantly, or had he suffered? Was there even anything left to bury? It was a gruesome thought, and she shook her head to clear her mind of the image. But another one took its place.

Adultery.

She was in the arms of another man when she received the news. Had begged David to hold her throughout the night, the premonition of something fearful that drove her there coming to life. Or in this case, death. Her husband's death. She betrayed the man who had just lost his life in a senseless act of war. The weight of the betrayal pushed her shoulders into a deeper hunch. Now she was left with a . . .

Baby.

Her baby would be born without a father. The man who was the father was denying his child, adamant that Yuri take responsibility. But Yuri was lying in a morgue thousands of miles away. He would never be a father.

David immediately offered her money. As if that could bring her husband back. All he could think about was the financial impact. The man lived and breathed the almighty dollar. But he wasn't the one suddenly looking at a future without the love she planned to share with Yuri through their golden years. And she did want to spend the rest of her life with Yuri. Despite the affair, which she knew now was a huge mistake. Too little, too late.

Images passed through her mind as she envisioned their future. She would have had Yuri's children. They would have had his brown eyes, strong jaw, and even stronger determination. They would have moved out of the city to a suburb with a yard. He would have bounced them on his knees. Swung them on their back-yard swing sets, laughing with them as they giggled. Taught them to ride their bikes, beaming in success as he let go for the first time. Handed his keys to them when they passed their driver's tests. Smiled wide, hands on hips, as they drove off into the sunset. Walked their daughters down the aisle to marry the man of their dreams.

She and Yuri would have turned old and gray together. He would have played on the floor with their grandchildren. She would have read to them as they huddled together on the sofa.

Now that future was gone. Like dust in the wind. Why, oh why, had she fallen into David's arms? Would things have been different if she hadn't beguiled him from her rooftop? She should have run when she realized the dinner party was only for the two of them. It should have been clear to her. On reflection, she knew it was very clear, and she should have said no. She should have gone with Yuri on his trips instead of staying home. Should have followed him to the ends of the earth. Would her husband still be alive if she had stayed faithful to him? The pain deepened in her chest, stabbing so hard she could barely breathe.

She shifted as the sofa got uncomfortable. Leaving the blanket in a pile, she rose and made her way to her bed. Her cold, cold bed. Curling up under the covers, she let her tears roll, soaking her pillow, and prayed for sleep to take away her living nightmare. Her biggest regret was that she would never know the answers to her questions.

Chapter Eight

A press conference was called for ten a.m. It was five o'clock in Jordan, the end of the workday. David received the details of the bombing from Jonas, and Nathan informed the next of kin for the other two fatal victims, as well as the families of those who were injured. Two team members would be on their way home, after going first to Germany for a quick medical check. Jonas stayed in Jordan, and their crisis team was on their way to assist.

David stood behind the podium that was set up on the front steps of the One World Trade Center, the building towering high above him. The sun shined against the mirrored windows reflecting the blue sky and puffy white clouds. It was perfect weather for an outdoor press conference, despite the subject. Nathan stood at his right shoulder, with William at his left, and a security team surrounded them from behind. He looked out over the crowd of reporters, who had already heard the news, creating a buzz in the air as they waited for an official statement. A bundle of microphones was affixed to the podium, and cell phones were held high in the air, hoping to catch a hot mic moment. They were sensing that this was more than just a random bombing.

"Good morning, everyone." David opened his comments. "I'll make a brief statement and take just a couple of questions." He adjusted his stance. Cameras clicked as telephoto lenses zoomed in on his face. Others strained to hold their phones in focus. He held his gaze steady, his expressions practiced. He had to show just the right amount of emotion. The crowd hushed as they awaited his words.

"Just before eight a.m. Jordanian time, which is one o'clock here in New York, a team from Kingston Holdings was walking down a street in Amman, Jordan, when a car exploded, killing three team members and injuring three more. Other bystanders were also killed or injured. A rogue faction has claimed responsibility for the bombing. The fringe group has no association with, nor has been known to, Kingston Holdings in any way. Our team members were simply the victims of an indiscriminate act of violence by a here-to-fore unknown terrorist group.

"All next of kin of the deceased, and the families of the injured, have been notified. We will be flying those family members to Germany, where they will meet with their loved ones, once they are stable enough to be moved. The Jordanian government is assisting with this transfer, and Kingston Holdings will take care of all arrangements and expense.

"Our hearts and prayers are with the families, and we ask that you respect their privacy at this time of grief and loss."

"Mr. Kingston! David!" Several reporters shouted, but David ignored them. He chose, instead, to acknowledge a woman in the front who stood with her hand in the air. She had been hand chosen by his PR team to ask the first question.

"Mr. Kingston. We heard that one of your vice presidents was killed in the blast. Can you confirm that?"

"I can confirm that our vice president of foreign acquisitions, Yuri Yassin, was killed in the blast."

"What was your team doing in Jordan?"

"I'm afraid I'm unable to discuss that at this time." He pointed at another reporter.

"Are you working with the Jordanian government on a secret project?"

"As I just said, I am unable to discuss that at this time."

Another reporter shouted. "Was your team targeted?"

David shook his head. "The blast is under investigation. That is all the time I have. Thank you for coming."

He turned to walk away from the podium.

"Mr. Kingston! I heard that Yuri's wife is pregnant with your baby. Did you have him killed?" The voice was loud and accusing.

David was immediately surrounded by his security team and hustled into the building. His highly skilled contingent was well trained in detecting and mitigating potential threats, and a second team swooped in on the reporter, escorting him away from the conference.

David was protected as if he was the president of the United States and hustled away to the elevator that would take them to the seventy-third floor. His mind reeled at what the accuser had suggested. He didn't do it. He didn't even cause it. It was very clearly a terrorist attack. But he had intentionally sent Yuri into Jordan, knowing the risks. And that made him guilty.

His relationship with Elizabeth was private. Where in the world did the reporter get his information?

———

Nathan followed David to his office. The look on the attorney's face told him this would not be a pleasant conversation.

"Come in, Nathan. Have a seat." David pointed to the leather chair in front of his desk. He sat back in his own chair and remained calm, not willing to let anyone see how the question had shaken him.

William brought in two bottles of water, setting one on a coaster in front of David and handing the other to Nathan. The assistant closed the door as he left the room, understanding that this conversation must be completely confidential.

Nathan looked around before sitting. He crossed one ankle over his other leg, his hands also crossed over his chest. The ankle made him look nonchalant, but his crossed arms were demanding, and his eyes were expectant.

"That was an interesting press conference." Nathan tilted his head.

"We knew it wouldn't be easy." David cracked open the bottle and took a long swig. He had not slept since the early morning phone call from Jonas. Dark circles hid under the light coat of makeup his stylist had applied before the presser. He always looked in command, no matter the situation.

"What's going on, David?" Nathan had a parental expression on his face, one eyebrow cocked. Like he had just caught his son covered in mud.

"Have you ever had this feeling, like there is something that you know, and you know that you know it, but you can't remember what it is?" David tilted his executive chair. The custom built, Moroccan leather, fully cushioned chair cost more than most people spent on their monthly mortgage payment. And in New York, that was thousands.

"What are you talking about?" Nathan locked eyes with him.

"I'm missing something, and I don't know what it is. But I should."

"You are talking in circles. I think the stress is getting to you."

"You would be stressed, too, if one of your asset teams had just been blown away." David stood and paced the room.

"True. But are we talking about that? Or about Elizabeth?" David felt Nathan's eyes on him as he paced. "Yuri spent lots of time running around the world for you. Leaving his wife alone. And meanwhile you sit up here in your ivory palace taking advantage of the situation."

David returned to his seat. "Get to your point, Nathan."

"What does that reporter know?" Nathan's question was sharp.

He stood again and leaned over his desk, staring directly at his attorney. "You know how rumors get started. A reporter shouts a question, fishing, and others run with it as if it is gospel. I won't pander to that." He picked up the bottle of water and took another drink.

Nathan set his unopened bottle on the desk. David moved it to a coaster.

"Perhaps, what you're missing is your conscience talking to you." Nathan sat forward, grabbing David's attention. "Don't you think God knows what you've done? And do you really think He is going to let you get away with it? Without any accountability? I was at the gala. The sparks were shooting between you and Elizabeth all the way across the room. And you looked pretty cozy there by the wall for a few minutes. As if you were sharing secrets."

Nathan paused before continuing, and David felt the intensity of his judgment.

"The baby is yours, isn't it?"

"What baby?" He continued to play innocent. But Nathan pressed him.

"What if she decides to sue? You do not need a paternity suit. You really don't want that kind of publicity. But more than that, you willfully broke God's law."

"Great. Just what I need. A Bible-thumping attorney. I thought you guys were extinct." David leaned back again, letting the chair tilt fully.

"Aren't you a Christian too? You've built this business on a verse from Psalms." Nathan opened his arms wide to indicate the office around them.

"Look. Yuri hasn't announced any pregnancy. If there is a baby, you know it's his. He was home for a couple of weeks before he went to Jordan."

"I know about the affair, David. I talked to William."

They studied each other, neither ready to flinch. But then David did. He could never put anything past his attorney and friend.

"Why are you talking to my assistant? I'll fire him." David walked to his window to watch the traffic below. They all looked like little ants, marching to their holes in the ground. Playing follow the leader. One by one. Two by two. But for what purpose?

"No, you won't fire him. You can't live without him. And besides, my job is to protect your interests. If that means keeping you out of trouble, I'll talk to William or whomever else I think necessary." Nathan flicked a piece of dust from his tailored suit pants.

"Nathan." David drew his colleague's attention back to his face. "We've been friends since college. We pulled a lot of pranks together. You were there for me when Abigail decided I wasn't enough. And again when Allison threw herself at that Wall Street tycoon. I bet she wishes she had stuck with me, now."

"Probably not." Nathan raised an eyebrow. "But if she had, you likely wouldn't be in this mess."

Nathan's words stung. Their eyes locked before David spoke. "Just do what you need to do, please. But remember. I hired you, and I can fire you." They both knew he would never do that.

"I'll need to bring in your PR team. They were there and heard the question, too. We need damage control. In fact, they are probably already working on it."

"No PR. Just do your job. If we handle it right, it will go away." David stared at him, his gaze firm. He had not admitted guilt. But they both knew the problem and the cost.

Nathan stood and left the room, and David shut the door behind him. Making his way to his sofa, he collapsed on the cushion and rubbed his hand over his face.

How did the reporter learn of the affair? Or was it just a guess? Very few people knew about the pregnancy. Himself, Nathan, William. And of course, Elizabeth.

Wait. The bartender at the gala. He traded Elizabeth's drink for water with lemon. And bartenders were usually pretty astute.

What was he going to do?

———

Elizabeth watched the press conference on her television, wincing when she heard the question shouted at the end. She was just now entering her second trimester and still had several months to go in her pregnancy. Would this scandal follow her around? How could she even show her face on the city street? She was afraid the paparazzi would stalk her but didn't know what to do.

She had loved Yuri. What happened to make their marriage fall apart? As she reflected on the past year or so, the signs were there. Yuri was gone more and more often, traveling as far as possible, for as long as possible. Was he doing that to please his boss? Or was he just trying to escape life at home?

Had she done something to drive him away? He couldn't possibly have known about her weekend visits to David. It all started to unravel long before then. His absence was what drove her into David's arms. It was ironic. Yuri's devotion to serving David had sent her straight to him.

Yuri talked about money. Making enough to retire young. Questioning him about it had fueled anger. He started out as a property manager, but quickly moved up the ranks to a position of great power. What was his goal? How much money was enough? Or did he want more than money? Did he want to acquire the company from David, the way David had from Antoni? And did his recent phone calls and dinners have anything to do with it?

It didn't matter because now he was dead. His climb up the corporate ladder had ended in the blink of an eye. Swiftly, abruptly, and painfully. And Elizabeth was left with a baby on the way and a heart twice broken.

———

Yuri's funeral was the following week. It was a small graveside service with only a few people in attendance. David. Antoni, and three other board members she didn't recognize. One was introduced as James, another Grayson. The third was a politician. A couple of other attendees said they were his friends. She didn't know them, but they were dressed in pricey suits. She was beginning to wonder just how much she didn't know about her husband. There were things she would never learn, now.

Trinity Church Cemetery was located in the Financial District. It was expensive to place the urn containing Yuri's ashes in the small vault only a cubic foot in size. But Yuri worked hard to gain his wealth, and in spite of how much he left her alone, she wanted to do right by him. And she felt he would like to be buried here, alongside founding fathers, inventors, and other famous people.

They were standing inside a small blue tent which sheltered them from the threatening rain, as well as prying eyes. She was grateful for the privacy. There was no media allowed, and several men in black suits stood outside the perimeter of the small group. Some looked like members of the security team that surrounded David after the news conference. Of course. He would need protection from the sharks.

The preacher began his eulogy. They were the standard he-was-a-good-man words from someone who didn't even know him. He loved his wife. He was a good employee, dedicated to his work. He gave to charities.

Wait. He did? Elizabeth should have paid closer attention to their finances.

She stared ahead as the preacher droned about her husband's life. The black marble container sat on a small velvet-draped table in front of the vault, where it would be sealed. Shaped like a vase that would hold flowers, bands of rich copper wrapped around the bottom of the urn, as well as the shoulder, or widest part of the vase. Ornate geometric designs were carved into the marble and inlaid with more copper. The cap was also marble, accented with a small copper band. It was a work of art.

This is what his life had been reduced to.

She loved her husband. She really did. But his hard work and constant travel were now defined by a few words prayed over an eight-by-ten-inch vessel. Tears spilled from her eyes, and she retrieved a tissue from her small black clutch to dab them away.

A drizzle fell from the sky as the minister said, "Amen." He laid a hand on her shoulder and expressed his condolences. The others filed by one at a time, offering a few words that meant nothing to her. David appeared at her side with an umbrella, his subtle cologne reminding her of their nights together.

"Would you like a ride back to your apartment?"

"No, thank you. I'll walk. It isn't far." She started to leave, but he stopped her with a hand on her arm.

He looked at her like he might argue, then simply shook his head. He had also attended the funerals of the other victims and arranged limo transportation for all the family members. They graciously accepted his offer. But not Elizabeth.

"Then please take my umbrella. I will have two of my guys escort you."

"That's not necessary. I'll be fine."

"Yes, it is. For your safety."

She studied his face. His eyes were sincere. Nodding once, she took the umbrella and left the cemetery, leaving him standing there in the rain. As lonely as she had been lately, today she needed the solitude. The light rain left puddles on the sidewalk and quickly soaked her shoes and the hem of her designer raincoat, making her shiver. She should have accepted David's offer to ride in his car.

Half a block away, she saw the reporters coming. One had a long-range camera. Had he been taking pictures of her during the funeral? She lowered her umbrella to hide her face, the Kingston logo shining brightly against the black cloth. Cameras snapped like a machine gun. She hadn't realized the logo would be there.

"Mrs. Yassin! Elizabeth! Can we get a statement?"

Fury rose in her veins. How dare they? As she buried her husband? She turned her back on them, but the footsteps came faster.

"Elizabeth! We've heard rumors that you were with another man when Yuri died. Do you care to comment?"

Savages. These paps weren't reporters. They were vultures. And how would they have known that, anyway?

"Mrs. Yassin! We see you have Mr. Kingston's umbrella. What is your relationship with him?"

One of the security guards stepped between her and the cameras.

"Back off, gentlemen. The lady just buried her husband. Give her some privacy, please."

A limousine pulled up to the curb, and the second guard took her elbow and guided her to it. The door opened, and he helped her inside.

"I was afraid that would happen." It was David.

He took her elbow to help her scoot in while the guard closed the umbrella. Both guards hopped quickly into the car, one in the front, the other in the back with her and David, and they sped away. She was furious at David for following her, but thankful for the intervention. Still, she wondered how the press would spin the encounter.

———

A few days later, her phone buzzed with a number she didn't recognize. After the funeral, Carlos, David's driver, had taken them straight to her elevator, which was hidden inside her building's garage. No reporters followed them. David said a simple goodbye and watched until the elevator door was closed. She finally felt like she could breathe.

Since then, she'd tried to calm her anxiety by binge-reading on her tablet to keep out the world. The stories were sappy, but they kept her from thinking about her current situation. And they kept her away from the social media sites. But eventually, her curiosity got the better of her, and she had to look.

One celebrity-sighting website posted a picture of her being shoved through the door into David's limo. The caption said she had a breakdown after the funeral and he rescued her. Breakdown, indeed. She wanted to pummel them.

Another site posted a picture of the opened umbrella pointed at the camera. The Kingston logo stood out like a confession about where she was spending her time and who she was spending it with. Additional photos tried to peer into the back seat as the limo sped away, but the images were blurry. Still, the implications were there. Leaving the funeral of her husband to rendezvous with another man.

Now, her phone was ringing with an unknown number. Fearful it would be someone from another trashy magazine, she ignored the call and let it roll to voicemail. In barely sixty seconds, a beep indicated a message had been left. Her finger hovered over the button. She wasn't sure she wanted to know what the caller wanted.

She wished she had sought out some friends when she moved to the city, but instead she'd spent her time taunting the man next door. She needed someone to talk to. But now she had no one to call. No one to offer her solace. Her family was in Israel, and she rarely spoke to them.

She finally touched the button to play the recorded message.

"Mrs. Yassin. This is Nathan Shepherd. Mr. Kingston's attorney. Please call me at your earliest convenience."

Elizabeth raised an eyebrow as she listened to the missive. David had done everything he could to ignore her. With the exception of his actions at the funeral, he acted like there was no relationship between them. Like the child in her womb didn't pulse with the blood and DNA of one of the most powerful man in the city. In the world, really, since he was so widely diversified. You didn't have to be in politics to be powerful. Money spoke much more loudly.

She wondered what he would offer. Yes, she knew there would be an offer to settle. And all it took was one question shouted from a reporter. Despite his kind behavior at the cemetery, David was in damage control mode. The offer would most likely include a clause absolving him of any responsibility for the child and a gag order for her silence.

She wasn't sure what she wanted. But she called the attorney and made an appointment with his assistant to meet him the next day.

CHAPTER NINE

ELIZABETH'S STOMACH flipped as she entered the elevator to the forty-second floor of the tall spire. She placed her hand over her abdomen, the move a protective reflex that she tried to curb, afraid it would give her away. The bile rose, then settled.

Her ears popped as the car made its rapid ascent. She remembered her ride to the seventy-third floor to deliver her pregnancy announcement. The dizziness of the sharp ascent followed by the subtle sway of the building at that height had brought on an unfortunate round of nausea. She had rushed to the ladies' room after William delivered her to the lobby.

Today, she rubbed her ears and flexed her jaw, snapping her mouth shut as the doors opened. A receptionist sat behind a welcoming counter just on the other side of a set of double glass doors with Nathan's name on the front. Taking a breath, Elizabeth walked through.

"I'm Elizabeth Yassin. I have an appointment to meet with Mr. Shepherd."

The receptionist was young and beautiful, with short brown hair curling over her ears. Her green silk blouse enhanced the green of her eyes. They looked like the finest Columbian emeralds.

"Welcome, Ms. Yassin. Mr. Shepherd is waiting for you in his office. This way, please." The woman led Elizabeth down a short hallway.

When she entered, Nathan rose to meet her, squeezing her hand in his as he did.

"Mrs. Yassin. I am so sorry for your loss."

She nodded, unsure of her voice or of the attorney's intent. She remembered seeing him at the gala, but they had not been introduced. She sat in a cushioned leather chair in front of his desk. The whisper soft chair sat next to a small round table, where he placed a bottle of water. Twisting off the cap, she took a long drink. Nathan waited quietly while she quenched her nerves.

Finally, she set down the bottle, and Nathan spoke. "Let me start by saying you have our sincere condolences. Yuri was a valued employee at Kingston Holdings and well-liked by everyone here."

Elizabeth didn't know what to say. That he was liked by everyone stung a bit. He put more of his efforts into his relationships with them than he did with her.

"The company will ensure that you will be well cared for as a result of Yuri's death. In addition to the substantial life insurance benefits that you will receive, we have established a trust fund that will provide a significant income for the rest of your life."

"Thank you. That's very kind." She waited for him to continue, certain there was more.

Nathan cleared his voice.

"I'm sure you saw the press conference."

"Yes, and I heard the question shouted by a reporter at the end." She finally found her voice. "I also had questions shouted at me the day of the funeral. After I had just buried my husband." Her anger at the actions of the reporters still seethed.

"Mr. Kingston is greatly concerned about the impact of those insinuations on you, and on your pregnancy."

Elizabeth looked at the man, trying to determine his sincerity. "How did you know I'm pregnant? How does anybody know? I haven't told anybody."

"Are you saying you aren't?"

"No." She lowered her eyes, scratching her fingers with her manicured nails. "Only that I haven't told anyone. Except David."

"I see." Nathan focused on her, quietly observing for a moment.

"Mr. Kingston would like to establish you in the location of your choice, away from New York, where you can enjoy your privacy. Away from the paparazzi. Perhaps you have family somewhere. Or you have someplace you have always wanted to live. A trust fund will also be established for your child. You will never want for anything again, Elizabeth." The compassion in his voice was unexpected and almost caused her to lose her focus.

"Except a father for my baby." She spoke calmly, but firmly.

"In return," he continued, "you agree not to discuss your pregnancy with the media or anyone other than your medical team, which will also be provided for you."

Did he not hear what she just said? Who would be the father to her baby?

"He's trying to buy me off. I knew he would do this." She pinched her eyes shut and clinched her fists around the arms of the chair, trying to control her emotions and her words.

"He's providing reasonable care for you and your child in light of the fact that your husband was killed while on company business."

"He wants to get rid of me. And our baby."

"He is concerned for your safety."

"Concerned?" She slapped her hands on the arms of her chair. "If he was truly concerned, he would be acknowledging this child as his." She placed her hands over her abdomen. "But instead, he wants to ship us far away so that he doesn't have to take responsibility for his actions."

"Do you really want the media hounds to follow you around, sticking cameras in your face everywhere you go? Do you want that for your child? The insinuations and lies they will fabricate about you?"

She bit her lip. He had a point, but she didn't want him to know that. What kind of life would she be giving her child if she stayed here? Was she unwilling to leave because she wanted her baby to have the father he or she deserved? Or was it because she secretly hoped David would want her in the bargain? She was a widow. If they wanted to have a relationship now, what did it matter to anyone else?

David needed to man up. Was she willing to fight back? To force him to do that? And if she did, would she win the battle, but lose the war? Would her baby suffer for it in the long run?

What kind of future would her child have? Would he be welcome in the highest social circles, or would he be scorned? Would he attend elite schools and be surrounded by many friends, or would he be ostracized? Would he be bullied for not having a father? Or would it make him stronger?

"Elizabeth. You have to see that David wants the best for you. Let him set you up somewhere. Yuri talked a lot about going to Hawaii. It is sunny and warm most of the year. Wouldn't you would like to have a home there?"

Hawaii? That was five thousand miles from New York. He really did want to get rid of her. It would be an easy solution because he had property there. Hadn't Yuri told her that? Then a thought occurred to her. Did David want to set her up as his mistress? A family hidden far away from his friends? He would visit two or three times a year, if that. She had heard stories of other men having secret families stashed away. She huffed and stood, glaring at Nathan.

"What if I don't want to leave New York? What if I want David to accept full responsibility for our child? A DNA test will prove paternity. And I'm thinking of suing for wrongful death, as well." Her anger grew.

"You don't really want to do that." Nathan's voice remained calm. "I suggest you sign the agreement. That will allow us to all move on." He looked at her as a father would look at an errant child.

Elizabeth glanced around the lavish office. She found a picture on a bookcase of a woman and young girl. Nathan's arm was draped around his wife's shoulders, his brown hair expertly styled, hers laying in waves over his arm. His other hand rested on his daughter's shoulder as she sat in front of them. The child looked just like her mother, with blonde hair and blue eyes. The family was all smiles.

"Is this your family?"

"Yes. My wife and daughter."

"And is this how you would want your daughter to be treated?" She pierced him with another glare. He didn't respond, his face bland.

The answer was suddenly clear. "Mr. Shepherd, I appreciate your time and efforts on my behalf. But we both know you are representing David's best interests, not mine. I think I need my own attorney."

She stood regally and left Nathan's office. Reaching the elevator, she sent a quick text message while waiting for it to respond.

"Your insulting offer is declined."

Then she sent a second message.

"Grandfather. We need to talk."

———

David walked into his mentor's office on the thirty-first floor of the Chrysler Building, discouraged. He began working with Antoni when he first arrived in New York, and the man continued as a friend and board member after David bought out his original company. Now Antoni owned twenty-five percent of Kingston Holdings. Between the two of them, no one else could overrule their decisions.

"David." Antoni stood and shook his hand. "It's nice to see you. But you look like a wreck. How about some coffee?"

"Coffee would be great. Thank you." David sat in the leather chair in front of Antoni's desk. He scrubbed his hand over his face, knowing he could be himself here with his old friend.

"You must admit it has been a long week. The media wants more info about why we are in Jordan, to start with. Are we cutting a deal with the devil?" A young woman entered with two cups of coffee. The nutty aroma lifted David's spirits as he accepted the cup. Antoni smiled and thanked her.

"We need the government's blessing if we want to do business there." David took a sip of the rich black beverage, approving of the blend.

"Granted. I just wonder if we are dealing with the wrong people." The elder man had decades of experience.

David picked up a picture of Antoni and a young girl that was sitting on his mentor's desk. He glanced briefly at it, then put it down. It was an old picture.

"Jordan sits on the Dead Sea, which is a prime source for brine and hard rock. Essential for development of lithium. We will be the first in the region, once we get the permits. But Israel is on the other side of the sea. And I have family there. Wouldn't you rather work with them?" Antoni turned the picture slightly toward his own view, smiling softly at the image.

"You have family in Israel? How did I never know that?" David paused before continuing. "Hamas has stepped up their bombings there. It would not be a safe place to build right now. Jordan would be a better option, despite what just happened." He drummed his fingers on the arm of his chair. "I hoped to keep this under wraps."

"Agreed." Antoni nodded. They needed to keep the deal quiet until the ink was dry. "Let's make up a story to give to the press about why we are there. We could be exploring properties for a new hotel. In fact, we should actually do that. It would give credibility to our presence."

"Unfortunately, Yuri was the man for that job." David shifted in his seat. "I'll talk to Jonas about it."

Antoni nodded again. But David didn't like the quizzical look his mentor was giving him.

"So, tell me more about the question fired off at the end of the press conference. Where did the reporter get that idea?"

David waved his hand. "Oh, you know the press. They are always shouting random questions, hoping something will stick." He stood and paced to the corner window, where a view of the stainless-steel flying eagle wings protruded from the ledge of the floor below them. The Chrysler Building was the tallest building in the world before the Empire State Building surpassed it eleven months later. It was a short-lived dream. Man is always trying to outdo himself. Now, several buildings around the world soared into the heavens. Like One World Trade Center.

"Stick? Like spaghetti on a wall?" David startled at Antoni's statement, then turned and laughed. He almost admitted to the accusation. His friend would understand.

"So, there is no truth to the rumor?"

Antoni had a strange look on his face. Something between hopeful and scheming, which made David think again. Looking his mentor straight in the eye, he responded with certainty.

"None whatsoever."

———

The private investigator entered the room and sat in the chair that David had just vacated.

"Did you get everything?"

"There wasn't much in the conversation, but yeah. I got it." The PI flipped his phone over in his hand.

Antoni pointed at the picture on his desk. "Can you get his DNA from that?"

"You handled the picture, too?" He pocketed the phone.

"Yes, unfortunately."

"Then no. We probably can't use that."

Antoni looked around his office and thought of the coffee cup. He buzzed his assistant.

"Have you already washed the coffee cups?"

"Sir? No. I haven't."

"Bring them both back in here, please."

Thirty seconds later, the buxom blonde returned with both coffee cups. Antoni picked up his, which contained the logo from his alma mater, and nodded to the other cup.

"He drank from that one."

"We normally want a cheek swab, but if you are trying to do this without his knowledge, that option is out. I think we can make this work, although there may be chain of evidence questions since the cup left this room." The investigator removed gloves and an evidence bag from his pocket.

"I need answers as soon as possible. The future of one of my prime companies is at stake. And you can use the touch DNA from the picture to validate the sample from the coffee cup."

"I can ask for a rush, but that will cost extra. We use a private firm for such requests."

Antoni waved his hand. "I don't care what it costs. I just need to know if my granddaughter is carrying David's child."

CHAPTER TEN

ELIZABETH HELD her hand over her stomach, the fluttering inside barely there in the early weeks of her second trimester. It was a strange feeling, but one she found that she cherished. Her queasy stomach had calmed, and she no longer spent her mornings over the porcelain throne. But she still carried crackers in her purse and had stocked up on antacids.

She certainly had never intended to get pregnant, but now that she was, she was looking forward to the birth of her son.

Yes, she was having a son. The ultrasound was very clear.

If Yuri was still alive, he would have been thrilled. Until he counted the months and determined the child wasn't his. Then he would have been livid, and rightly so. And once he discovered who the father was, she could not imagine how he would have responded. Because the betrayal went far beyond her participation in the affair. David was not only his boss, but also his mentor and friend. Yuri practically worshipped the man. She recalled the adage about putting a person on a pedestal. They will eventually fall off.

She had always been faithful to Yuri. Always. How she had fallen, letting the loneliness of Yuri's travels get the best of her and allow her mind to wander, she didn't know. She hadn't set her sights on David, specifically. She supposed it could have been any one of the several men she knew had watched her from the building across the street. But David responded to her silent plea. Her silent game. Her silent taunts.

Now Yuri was gone. David was denying any plausibility. And the only man left in her life was still months away from taking his first breaths outside the womb.

She grew up in Israel. She met Yuri at the University of Tel Aviv, where he attended as a foreign student. They moved to America not long after their marriage, when Yuri had gotten his first position in David's company. He moved up the ladder quickly, applying his education and skills, but mostly by learning from the master himself.

She could always go home. Her parents would welcome her and her child, and David's settlement would help establish her there. But she had grown to like New York. She wanted to continue her life here, despite everything.

When a growling sound emitted from her stomach, she laughed to herself. The child inside her belly was constantly hungry. She walked to the refrigerator, took out a couple of boiled eggs and a bagged salad for a quick meal, then put them back in. She wanted something different. Was this what everyone meant when they talked about cravings?

She pulled a jar of pickles from the fridge then crossed to her cabinet for a jar of peanut butter. Opening both, she forked a pickle and dipped it in the gooey peanut goodness. The tangy pickle mixed with the earthy peanut on her tongue, and she closed her eyes in delight. Oh, that flavor was intensely good. Hopefully by eating peanuts now, her child would not be born with the dangerous peanut allergy.

She had not talked to her attorney about suing David or the company, or accepting his offer. Yuri left plenty of money in his bank accounts, and he had multiple investments. She would be able to continue in her current lifestyle with very few changes. To start a court battle, especially in the middle of her pregnancy, might bring more trouble than it was worth. But she had plenty of time to figure that out.

She did want to seek out new friendships. She could find a social club to join or get involved with some philanthropic organization. Anything to fill her time and refocus her energies. And take her mind off David. She finished her pickle and tossed the fork into her sink.

An itchy, burning feeling crawled across her skin, her belly suddenly tight. Was she having a reaction to her weird snack? She lifted her blouse to inspect the pain and found redness there, but no hives like she might have expected. Rubbing her tiny baby bump, she located her skin lotion in the bathroom and squirted a small dollop. The lotion soothed her skin, but not the tightness that also burned through her soul. What did her future look like, and that of her child?

She would need a nursery. Stepping into her office, she perused the layout and determined it would work if she moved her desk to the back side of the room. She could then put a crib, chest of drawers, and changing table on the side nearest the door. A stack of mail sat on her desk. She would send the bills to her accountant. Spying another business magazine, she tossed it in the trashcan. She would also need to cancel those subscriptions.

Continuing her mental list, she picked up her laptop and took it with her into her living space. Plopping onto the sofa, she opened a notes app and began her list.

A car seat would have to be bought, first. The hospital wouldn't let the baby come home without inspecting and approving the seat. Browsing an online catalog, she was astounded at the options. Everything from a hundred dollars for a basic seat with straps, to much more complex and accessorized models. A luxury version had built-in airbags and sensors that connected to the car via Bluetooth. It would even monitor the internal temperature in the car and notify via cell phone of any imminent danger to the baby. Travel systems that grew with a baby teetered at two thousand. This, for a child that would spend a few months at most in it. And she didn't even have a car. How was that supposed to work? She closed her laptop and set it aside.

The morning sun shone through the buildings across the street to cast a beam on her floor. Was God in that beam? She remembered that as a child, she used to think that God was shining His love through the window. Was He smiling on her today? Or were those simply floating dust motes, and nothing more? Wandering her apartment, she reached Pete's cage. He ruffled his feathers in greeting.

"There is going to be a new member of our family soon."

"New friend."

"That's right." She covered her abdomen with her hand and sighed. Before long, her apartment would be filled with the oohs, aahs, and cries of a newborn. Would Pete be able to mimic those sounds? He was a very talented bird. No doubt he would be having conversations with the baby, and she wouldn't understand a word. She giggled at the thought.

She needed a friend. And clothes for her growing figure. She decided to check out a few local designers. A new wardrobe was the fix for everything.

———

Several weeks went by. There was no word from Elizabeth or her attorney, but she was suddenly busy on the social scene. Her pictures were splashed all over social media and entertainment shows. She wasn't showing, and she didn't talk about the baby. In fact, she partied like she wasn't pregnant. David wondered if she had ended her impending motherhood. The thought both relieved him and made him sick.

He instructed Nathan to go ahead and establish the trust fund for her due to Yuri's death, but he was worried. The silence from her was shouting at him.

He crossed the tarmac at the private airstrip and boarded one of his two private jets for the long flight to Jordan. The Dassault Falcon 8X had often carried Yuri and his teams to their many site visits, offering flexibility they couldn't find with commercial flights. It had most recently been used to transport the victims of the bombing and their families back to their respective homes.

Taking a seat at one of the conference tables, he buckled his seatbelt and prepared for flight, leaning back in the sumptuous chair. The soft, lambskin leather was hand-stitched. The company logo, a crown over the letter K, was sewn into the seat back, as well as the cushioned leather on the front bulkhead. Even the carpet contained the logo, in a custom woven pattern of varying shades of gray with red accents. They were his favorite colors.

The pilot's voice came over the intercom. "Good morning, Mr. Kingston. We are clear for takeoff whenever you are. Skies are clear, and the flight across the pond should be smooth."

Good. He was meeting Jonas and a couple others over there. He would need to be well-rested for this final phase of negotiations. He nodded at the flight attendant, and soon they were high over the Atlantic Ocean, the city skyline fading away behind them.

"Would you like a drink, sir?"

"I'll take my normal, please."

The blonde flight attendant had served for several months and knew his standing orders. She was a very pretty woman and implied on more than one occasion that she found him attractive. In other circumstances, he might have taken her up on her unspoken offer. After all, the jet was fully equipped with a master suite. But his brain reneged, conjuring up the dark hair and eyes that haunted his sleep nearly every night. He pulled his tablet out of his satchel and opened his social media account.

He felt like a stalker. He had set up a pseudo account and followed Elizabeth as she moved from party to party, event to event. Dressed in glamorous gowns, she was seen on occasion with one of his board members. A pop-up notification flashed a picture of her with Antoni, and it turned his stomach. He was kissing her cheek.

The man was old enough to be her father. Then again, David was twenty years her senior. He hadn't even noticed the age gap. From the expression on his face, Antoni didn't, either.

Her gown shimmered like fine gold. It fit snugly over her hips in an intricate pattern of pleats and gathers, flaring just above the knees into tiny pleats that fell to the floor. The bodice danced with gold beads, the neckline bold and daring. He would love to shower her with diamonds. Canary yellow to grace her neck, and more to dangle enticingly from her ears.

He could reach out to his friends from Sierra Leone, where he owned a stake in a diamond mine. Or he could go with lab diamonds, but Elizabeth should be wearing the real thing. Never mind the labor used in the diamond mines. It provided jobs, didn't it?

He couldn't remember the last woman he bought jewels for. Was it his mother? Or one of his former wives? It had been that long ago. Perhaps he should make some time to swing down to the mine after completing his deal in Jordan.

"Is there anything I can get for you, Mr. Kingston?" The flight attendant's smile beckoned to him, and she boldly put her hand on his shoulder.

He laid the tablet face down on the side table, realizing he was daydreaming. There was no relationship with Elizabeth. He didn't have the right to shower her with diamonds. And she was flaunting that fact by stepping out with other men. She wasn't even mourning Yuri. She deserved the right to do this, given all the circumstances. He shook his head, startled at where his thoughts had gone, and focused on the present. Here and now.

"What would you suggest?" He gazed at the blonde, considering his options.

"You seem tense. I would be happy to rub your shoulders. I am a certified masseuse."

"It will be a long flight, and I have work to do. Perhaps follow up with me in a couple of hours?" Her perfume smelled like a summer breeze.

"Certainly. Enjoy your flight." Her hand lingered before she turned and made her way up the aisle, the split in the back of her short skirt providing a hint of promise.

His eyes went back to his tablet, and more pictures. An astute observer had drawn a circle around Elizabeth's abdomen.

Chapter Eleven

"Grandfather. Did you see the picture? Did you see what they did to it? How dare they? Can't I enjoy some peace and privacy?" Elizabeth paced across her bedroom, switching her phone from one ear to the other.

"Not when you are flaunting yourself around town. I enjoyed escorting you to the theater, but you need to start thinking about how you will explain the baby bump as it grows."

"I have a friend back home who barely showed at all until she was almost seven months. If I start showing now, I'm going to look like a cow. And I won't be able to wear the designer dresses that I'm being paid to wear. It's a great gig. Beautiful gowns for free. All I do is prance around at an event and impress the right people." She glanced at the tablet she tossed onto her dresser, frustrated at the pictures that were being posted on social media.

"Have you told the designer?"

She started working with Leoni a month ago, after seeing her designs on a Broadway star as she walked the red carpet. The star had given Leoni a special mention in her comments to the reporters. Reaching out to the designer, she found the woman to be warm, inviting, and her designs really appealed to Elizabeth. Classic, classy, and still modern. She would have paid Leoni's price, but the deal was a good one, and it included invites to social events due to Leoni's existing network. She was quickly developing a friendship with the woman.

"No, I haven't told her. And I'm not going to until it becomes noticeable."

"Do you think this designer could create a dress around the pregnancy? You should be honest with her."

Elizabeth sighed and flopped onto her bed. "I don't know. It's worth considering. But the last thing I need is for people to start thinking that reporter was right. I can't end this pregnancy, even though it's still legal in New York. I won't end it. But sometimes I wish it would go away."

"Don't invite trouble, Elizabeth. You should be making plans for yourself and the baby. The child is going to change your life. Permanently. You can't ignore that."

She was well aware of that, but not ready to think through all the logistics of having a baby. Insurance. Diapers. Onesies. Breast-feeding versus bottles. Childcare. School. She knew some preschools booked years in advance, especially here in the city. It was over-whelming.

"I'll get a nanny. And I should go ahead with that lawsuit."

"I would not sue him, yet. I have some ideas that will get the revenge you need without upending your world. Give me some time."

"Okay, Grandfather. You are usually right, so I will follow your advice. But can we please arrange a non-disclosure agreement with the designer? I would love to see what she can come up with that will hide the baby as long as possible." Her maid already had an NDA agreement in place, part of her package when she was hired. Her designer needed one, too.

"Of course I'm right. And yes, I'll have my attorney draw up the agreement. You deserve beautiful gowns. Perhaps, it's also time to start working on your own clothing line."

Her stomach tumbled, and her hand automatically went there.

The quiver reminded her every day of her choices. With David, and now.

"I think I'll stay with my current plan. And I need that agreement as soon as possible."

Her grandfather chuckled from the other end of the phone call. "Of course, my dear."

Elizabeth ended the call, sighed, and collapsed into a chair at her dining table. Pete fluffed his feathers as she did.

"Pretty lady."

She looked up at her bird. "Thanks, Pete." She could always count on her faithful pet.

———

David eyed the men sitting around the table in the executive board room. Six wore the robes of the Arab elite. They were smiling and laughing, knowing they had the upper hand in the negotiations. They had something that David wanted. And he would have to determine how to deliver whatever they would ask for in order to get them to sign off on the deal.

Jonas and three others flanked him on his side of the table, all men, since women were not permitted in the meetings. Voice activated microphones were embedded in the table in front of them, their red and green lights indicating when they were live and recording. He had been in similar discussions, but this one was more critical in nature. He had already lost three men, and three others were injured, including two women. His gut told him that had been a warning shot.

David knew he was walking a fine line by dealing with Jordan instead of Israel. He tried to have peaceful relationships with everyone he dealt with, but when trade agreements clashed due to politics, the negotiations could be tenuous.

Jordan was asking for arms as part of the compensation package for access to the Dead Sea. He could not legally do that, nor would he. He wouldn't give them something they could then turn on any of his other trading partners. David thought the request was probably just a test, anyway. International contracts always had kinks, and each country had their own rules and customs.

"Gentlemen. We have a new offer." This was their second trip to the table.

He nodded at Jonas, who clicked a key on his laptop. The large monitor at the end of the room displayed pictures of the proposed land deal, followed by numbers and graphs indicating how the deal would be beneficial to both parties. The presentation ignored the request for arms.

"This is all well and good. Very impressive. But you have agreements with our friends to the west. Do their agreements include arms?" Sheikh Abdullah led the discussion.

"I don't deal in arms. Period."

"How about women? I have seen a beautiful woman on the social media pages lately. I believe she was the wife of one of the men that was killed in the bombing. Yuri was your envoy, was he not?"

David nodded, keeping his face neutral.

"She is fascinating. Suave and graceful. I would like to meet her." The sheikh's smile was almost a smirk.

David furrowed his eyebrows together. "I don't think that will be possible."

"You speak for her? She has the look of an Arab princess. I could make her very happy. And she must be very lonely, now that her husband is gone." It was a taunt.

He stalled. Jonas looked at him quizzically. The other men sat quietly. This was unexpected.

"She is still mourning her husband."

The sheikh smiled thinly. "Then she should not be splashed all over your Internet. You Americans must have more control over your women." The jab was clear.

Jonas sent a quick text from his phone. David glanced at the ping.

"We will have to table these discussions for now. An urgent matter has just come to my attention. Shall we regroup later?"

"You have three days, gentlemen. Otherwise, the deal is off."
The six sheikhs stood, all following Abdullah from the room.

———

He wasn't going to dial. He wasn't going to ask. He knew she would immediately disconnect the call, sending it back into cyberspace and likely blocking his number. But he had to say he had at least tried. He would tell the sheikh he reached out, but that she declined the invitation. It would be partially true, and much easier than denying him flat out. Even if it did give him indigestion.

David flipped the phone over in his hand and looked at Jonas, where he and the team gathered around the small conference table in David's suite at the exclusive hotel. His head throbbed, the pain pounding in his temple.

"He's just trying to see how serious we are about the deal. He doesn't really want to meet Elizabeth, does he?" Jonas asked the question, but the faces of the other four men held the same inquisitive look.

"We made a good offer. If he doesn't agree, we will walk away. Israel has access to the Dead Sea from the western shore. It will be more dangerous because of the proximity to the West Bank, but it will be a better option if the sheikhs won't play ball." He pinched his forehead and temple between his thumb and fingers.

"I have concerns about the car bomb, anyway. I get the feeling it was meant for us, but I don't know why. There is an undisguised faction that doesn't want us in Jordan. But is it them, or is it someone else?" Jonas was just a few yards behind the team when the bomb went off.

"Jordan has agreements with all its neighbors, including Israel. Although that one is tenuous, at best. But that doesn't mean the neighbors want us to be there."

"Why don't we walk away while we are still alive?" One of the other men, Thomas, had spoken.

"We will see what they say in three days. Our current offer

stands. We won't negotiate further." David started to stand. It was time for supper, and his stomach was growling fiercely. A nice steak would fix that.

Thomas tilted his head and tapped a finger on the table.

"What's on your mind, Thomas?"

"I don't understand the whole Elizabeth thing."

"What do you mean?" David sat back into his chair and found himself frowning yet again. The others mirrored Thomas's question in their faces.

"Well, we looked her up. On social media. And I don't know about you, but she looks pregnant to me. I mean, that's the way my wife looked when she was about four or five months along."

The others nodded their heads.

"So when was Yuri home long enough for that to happen?" Thomas was always the doubter.

David laughed. "Man, you ought to know this. It only takes one time."

"Yeah, okay. But why would the sheikh be interested in her, then? I'm just having trouble connecting the dots."

All eyes looked back at David for his response. Had they heard of the reporter's insinuations? He did have her number in his phone. He suddenly realized he should probably have had William make the call.

"Women have been a pawn in this part of the world for centuries. They are like property. And my guess is the sheikh wants to add to his collection."

"He's not doing this to get back at you for something?"

"His attraction to her has nothing to do with me." David kept a straight face, looking Thomas in the eye.

The men looked doubtful. Did the sheikh also suspect his connection to Elizabeth?

Chapter Twelve

Elizabeth watched her designer take new measurements and tried not to place her hand over her stomach. She stood on a raised platform, about twelve inches above the floor of the room. Mirrors surrounded them, and the room smelled of the spicy incense of the Hindi. The woman clicked her tongue as she worked.

"When are you due?" The designer looked up into Elizabeth's eyes before looking down again at the yellow measuring tape that was wrapped around her hips.

"Excuse me? I'm not sure what you mean." The question threw her off guard.

"I know women's bodies. I have spent years designing beautiful clothes for us." She swept her hand over Elizabeth and herself. "I have designed gowns to hide pregnancies for many highly placed women. Women who don't want the world to know about their condition just yet. Or not at all. You have that look."

Should she tell her? The question invaded Elizabeth's thoughts. The woman looked sincere. And she had become a good friend in the past month. Could she be trusted? Elizabeth yearned for a confidant. Someone who would understand her fears and could share her hopes. She waited for Leoni to look up again before responding.

"Do you have any children?" She swallowed as she watched Leoni work.

"My husband and I have three beautiful daughters. And we have a grandchild on the way."

"You started your designer career later in life?"

"No. I worked at several design houses for a while until I met my husband. Then I took a break to focus on my family while they were young. I'm fortunate to have this opportunity to design for beautiful people at my age."

"You're not old." She must be around fifty with a grandchild on the way, but she didn't look to be over thirty. She wore her black, wavy hair in a twist to keep it out of the way, but her dark skin glowed with the look of high-priced creams, much like her own. And Elizabeth was only twenty-four.

"Old enough." Leoni winked.

"What made you want to be a designer?"

"Hm? Mmmm." Leoni removed one of the five straight pins she had just stuck into her mouth and made a fold in the dress.

Elizabeth fidgeted.

"Hold still, dear. I don't want to poke you with a pin." The designer spoke around the pins in her mouth.

"Sorry." She straightened, looking into the mirror. Black hair and dark brown eyes stared back at her, but she didn't feel like herself. This was all becoming a dream.

Leoni smiled. "I was four when I made my first dress."

"Four? As in, years old?"

The designer chuckled. "Yes, but not quite like you think."

"What happened?" Elizabeth looked down, then checked herself and straightened again. Leoni sat back on her feet before turning to sit fully on the platform. She patted the carpet beside her for Elizabeth to sit.

"I've always liked to play with pretty fabric. One day I got bored. My mother was doing something. I don't even remember what. But I went to her and asked if she could help me drape some fabric around me. I had cut an opening for the head and neck, and arm holes, and had a couple of clothes pins to help clip it together."

"Awe. That sounds adorable."

"Might have been. Except I used my bed sheets." Leoni winked and shook her head. "My father was not happy. He said we could barely afford bread, and here I was cutting up good sheets. So I had to sleep with only blankets until we could afford new sheets. But my mother . . ."

Leoni's voice got soft. Elizabeth laid her hand on her friend's arm, urging her to continue.

"My mother saw something in me. She went around to friends and tailor shops in the neighborhood and asked for scraps and gave them to me, with needle and thread. Then when I was six, I think, she bought a used sewing machine with money Father saved back, somehow. It was a small, portable Singer. And she taught me to sew."

"That is a beautiful story." Elizabeth squeezed back a tear, thinking of the tiny girl with a small sewing machine whose mother scrimped and saved to give her daughter a dream.

"Yes. We started taking in sewing, doing contract work for a couple of tailors. I worked right alongside my mother. I met a lot of people that way, and now, here I am." Leoni shrugged.

The two women stood, and Elizabeth swallowed. She would be having a baby soon. Could she build a life for her child like that? Her skin suddenly burned, and her hand went to her stomach.

"Since you have experience, may I ask you a question?"

The wiser woman tilted her head at Elizabeth. "Of course."

"My skin has been itching and burning. Do you have any special cream that I can use? I want to be very careful about introducing any chemicals to the baby."

Leoni smiled a half smile. "I will tell you what you need to do. It is an Old-World concoction, but it works."

"Thank you, Leoni."

"It is my pleasure. Now. Tell me. Do you plan to remain social throughout your term? Or will you go away for a while, as many women do?"

"I haven't thought that far ahead."

"I will design for you anyway. I will enjoy the challenge."

Elizabeth swallowed again. "I need you to sign a non-disclosure agreement."

"It's a little late for that, don't you think?" Leoni's eyes twinkled.

"I need complete privacy."

"Ah. Yuri is not the father, is he?" Leoni moved the tape again to measure her waist. The thickening flesh was starting to pinch her pants.

"A dead man cannot be a father."

Leoni gave her a knowing smile. Elizabeth surmised the designer had held many secrets about her clients over the years. Her phone buzzed, and she saw David's name displayed from where it sat on the orange sofa. Why was David calling? She stepped off the platform and hit the ignore button.

"I have what I need for today. Come back next week. I will have gowns ready for a first fitting." Leoni's words brought her attention back to the designer. But her mind wondered about the call.

———

"She declined your gracious offer." David and his team sat in the sheikh's boardroom again. This deal would either proceed today, or they would walk away. The cost of losing the access they wanted to the Dead Sea was already high. Three people were dead, three others flown home for convalescence and rehab. The men at the table agreed that being here was worth the risk, although they were now escorted to and from the office by a highly skilled—and expensive— security team. David was not concerned about his safety as he had no family back in New York, but some of his team members did.

Abdullah shrugged. "There are many more women in the world. I just wanted to see if you still had any integrity left."

David kept a straight face, while inwardly he scrunched his eyes, twisting his lips to one side. "I strive for integrity in all my deals. My business is built on it."

"As you should. I need to know that whomever I am dealing with will not stab me in the back. You are American, after all. Our countries don't have the greatest of relationships. Now, if you would just give up this foolish support of Israel."

"I will deal with whomever will work with me fairly. Be it Jordan or Israel."

"Then let's give our agreement a twelve-month trial. With monthly reports sent directly to me."

The other sheikhs nodded their approval. They would never question Abdullah.

David's team also nodded. "I'll have our attorneys draw up the agreements. They will likely have a few red lines to work through. Hopefully we can meet next week for an official signing."

The men all shook hands. He could smell the victory.

———

"This gown is stunning, Leoni. I love the swirl of colors. And the style gives me room to grow while still being sleek. At least for the next couple of months." Elizabeth turned back and forth in front of the many mirrors.

"The cut accentuates your bosom, and the colors help hide your little bean."

Her hand automatically went to her stomach. "My little bean. He's a few inches long by now."

"And turning somersaults in your womb. Do you feel his flutters?" Leoni patted Elizabeth's bump.

"Oh, yes. It reminds me that I am carrying life, right here inside me." She marveled at the idea of her body growing a tiny person.

Leoni smiled. "You will be coming to Fashion Week, won't you? I would love to put you on the runway in this gown."

Elizabeth shook her head. "No runway, please. But I will wear the dress to the gala."

Leoni focused her gaze on Elizabeth. "You have two choices, child. You can hide away, lonely, until this baby is born. Or, you can face the world with your head held high, gracing every runway, event, and theater like a princess. Whether you wear my gowns or not. This baby may not have been conceived intentionally, but he is no accident. And the fact that you are his mother was also not a random choice. Of that, I am sure."

Elizabeth blinked her tears away.

"So, Fashion Week?"

"Yes, Leoni. I will walk the runway."

"And bring a plus one to the gala?"

"Of course." She considered her options of available men. She would likely run into David. She wanted him to know she had moved on, but she wasn't in a good place to do that. She would call her grandfather. He would know what to do.

Chapter Thirteen

The private jet waited on the tarmac. All signed agreements were delivered digitally to the board, with the hard copies in his satchel. His team would continue in Amman to begin the project.

The black SUV pulled up next to the jet. David stepped from one to the other, while the driver handed his bags to the flight attendant. The sumptuous plane smelled like home. He was only eleven hours away.

Settling in his seat and buckling the belt across his lap, he opened his tablet to check messages and emails and received an alert from his search engine. Elizabeth was walking the runway at New York Fashion Week? In her condition?

The dress was a knockout. The glittering swirl of red and gold accentuated her olive skin and dark eyes.

"Mr. Kingston, we are ready for takeoff. Can I get you anything before I go to my seat?"

It was the same flight attendant. Savannah? He thought back to the first flight to Jordan. She made a very tempting offer, but in the end, he declined. He was not interested in a new fling. Not after Elizabeth. He had learned something from this midlife crisis. And he was still learning.

The sheikh said he was testing David's integrity. If Abdullah knew the full truth, would they still have gotten the deal? David looked up at the young woman, who was glancing down at his tablet. He closed the cover.

"I'll take a bottled water after takeoff, please. Thank you."

The jet rose into the sky, and David opened his tablet again. Elizabeth. The dress fit her well, and if he hadn't known better, he would not have been able to tell she was pregnant. How far along was she? He itched to know.

The designer was very talented. He flipped through the pictures to find Elizabeth with a man. Antoni? Why was she with him again? Something wasn't sitting right in David's mind. It was like a name he was trying to remember that was right there on the tip of his tongue. Or like a deck of cards, missing the ace of spades. Close, but not quite complete.

He closed the tablet again, along with his eyes, and pushed a button to put his chair into a reclining position.

His team was suspicious, as was Abdullah. Although he had a signed contract, they seemed to be playing a game of hide and seek. Someone was waiting for him to make a noise that would give him away. Would he be found? Could he make it to home base in time? It was a silly child's game, but it had serious implications as an adult. He wiped his hand across his face, only to look up at the flight attendant, who had a strange look.

"Here is your water, sir." The attendant was all professional now, her implied invitations tucked snugly away for the next wealthy passenger. Had she finally realized he was not interested? Or was she having doubts about him too? What if she had seen the insinuating article on social media? And how many others had seen it?

———

Another week flew by. David stood in his conference room, his quarterly business review ready for the board. It had been a very successful quarter, and he had the numbers to show for it, along with the signed agreement to explore for lithium in Jordan. Stock prices were soaring, and everyone in the room was growing wealthier by the minute.

"This is all great news, David." The speaker was James, one of the less friendly of the board members, but still a necessary asset. "But explain to me why we are in Jordan, again? Isn't that a slap in the face to our friends in Israel?"

David surveyed the room. James and Grayson had both been board members for almost ten years. They had been new investors from old money and, until now, had never questioned any suggestion he made. James, his hair now salt-and-pepper, with green eyes that reminded David of a cat. Grayson, his hair and eye color matching his name. Both were fit and wore their suits well, but probably never touched a gym.

"We walk a fine line in the Middle East, that is true. And yes, we have business in Israel. But I like to cultivate relationships with people on both sides of an issue."

"Hedging our bets?"

"Straddling a fence?"

The questions didn't rattle him. "More like keeping your friends close and your enemies closer. Our initial surveys there are promising. We stand to make a lot of money if this pans out. And we are not as likely to get hit by flying shells from other Arab countries.

Antoni played with an ink pen, rolling it between his fingers. He tapped it on his notepad, and finally laid it down on the blank page. David waited for him to say something, but the man stayed quiet. That bothered him more than if his mentor would have spoken out in opposition.

A selection of lunch sandwiches and salads was catered from one of the delis in the building. This was not your typical bologna sandwich. The deli served only the freshest cuts, hand sliced for each sandwich. Cheeses came from France. Salad greens and other vegetables were sourced as locally as possible.

David selected his food, then his next words.

"Antoni. I have seen you on social media lately with Yuri's wife."

His mentor looked back at him. "She needed an escort recently. I offered my assistance. Is that a problem?"

"No problem here, but the sheikhs in Jordan saw her on their feeds, as well. They questioned why we didn't keep our American women under control. She should be mourning, not going to theaters, parties, and Fashion Week."

"What business is it of theirs?"

"It almost stopped negotiations. Abdullah wanted to meet her. I think he wanted to add her to his harem." It irritated him that the sheikh had even made the suggestion.

"And you told him no, I take it?" Antoni raised an eyebrow.

"I told him she graciously declined. Why was she with you, anyway? Aren't you a little old for her?" David took a sip of his iced tea and frowned. It was a little too sugary for him. He pushed the glass back and reached for his bottled water.

"I simply offered an elbow, and she accepted. Yuri isn't here anymore." Antoni shrugged, one hand raised in challenge.

"I'm aware of that," David snapped, miffed at Antoni's implication.

"Well, unless you have a better offer to make, I will be happy to stand by her side."

The other board members watched the exchange with interest. Lunch suddenly soured in David's stomach. What was he doing, anyway? He had no reason to comment on Elizabeth's social activities, or Antoni's. But he couldn't help that he chafed at them.

Antoni was mocking him. His friend and mentor was suddenly enamored of Elizabeth, and David didn't understand why. Nor was Antoni willing to offer an explanation. There was something he was missing. It eluded his brain, and that fact alone bothered him. He was always on top of every detail.

The sheikh had expressed interest. Granted, Elizabeth was a beautiful woman. And yes, they had their own fling for a few weeks.

But he had let her go and couldn't go back and lay claim now. Or could he? And if he did, how would she respond?

She would likely rip him to shreds, and she could easily do that. One word to the right person would make his stock tumble. He could not let his business suffer.

No, he would stick with the current plan. He created the trust to provide for the child. It would set the babe up for his entire life. That would be enough.

———

Elizabeth lay on the examination table while the doctor listened to the baby's heartbeat. Leoni had accompanied her to this appointment so that she wouldn't be alone. The two of them had become good friends.

"Everything looks good, Elizabeth. No gestational diabetes, and I know you are watching your diet. Blood pressure is good. Baby boy is growing normally and measures perfectly for six months. Ultrasound shows no abnormalities." The doctor patted her knee and helped her to sit up.

"You mentioned everything but my skin. Why is my skin itching and burning? It's as if I am having an allergic reaction to my baby." She hugged her stomach again as the burning returned.

"I want to run more tests. Right now, I'm calling it an idiosyncratic dermatological response to pregnancy." The doctor's eyes twinkled. "Basically, it means I have no idea. Could be hormonal, but we don't want to give you anything that would harm the baby. You may just have to ride it out."

She looked at Leoni, who was standing off to the side.

"You don't think it could have anything to do with the father, could it?"

The doctor laid his hand on her arm, his eyes kind. "I'm very sorry about your husband. And yes, stress can do a lot of things. Why don't you get dressed, and I'll have my nurse draw blood for the additional tests. Oh. And one more thing."

"What's that?"

"Our office received a call from a man named William, at Kingston Holdings. He said they would be guarantor for the patient portion of all your medical bills. Is that correct?"

Elizabeth scratched her hands, then her abdomen. David wanted to pay her bills?

"My husband worked for them."

"Yes. I forgot that. Okay then. We will file your insurance as we would normally and send any remaining portions to them, with a copy to you. I'll have you sign a form up front. I will also need you to update your HIPAA form. This will ensure that if we need to discuss your condition with anyone, we know your privacy preferences." His eyes filled with compassion, then he turned and left the room.

Leoni smiled. "Let's get a quick lunch, and you can tell me all about that little tidbit." She tilted her head. "Remember. I'm great at keeping secrets."

Elizabeth had no doubt. It made sense that her burning skin could be caused by stress. The doctor hadn't acted like anything was unusual about her questions. But Leoni had a gleam in her eye that said she saw more than she was letting on. No doubt Elizabeth would be spilling her guts to her new friend before long.

———

A few days later, Elizabeth rose to the wonderful earthy smell of her special blend coffee and heard the door click as the maid left at seven fifty-five. The woman was impeccable in her service, always on time like the tide, rolling in and out. Or the moon. Always there, orbiting the earth, even when it is on the other side of the horizon, unseen. Elizabeth would have to give her a raise.

"Good morning." The bird squawked.

"Good morning, Pete. How are you today?"

"Baby bump."

"What did you say?" She looked at her bird, wondering where he got his new words.

"Baby bump."

Her hand went to her growing mound. "Yes, the baby is growing."

"Bad baby."

She swiveled her head. "No. Good baby."

"Baby bump."

Elizabeth lowered the cover on the bird cage to stop Pete's chatter. What had her maid been teaching him? She sipped her coffee and stepped out onto the terrace. September was turning into October. The city blinked at her, the early morning lights going out as the sun rose in the sky. But the forecast called for clouds, with a possibility of snow flurries.

She wished she had trees around her, but at this height, all she saw were the surrounding buildings. Concrete and steel. Gray, gray, and more gray, with a little brownstone and red brick mixed in. She would have to take a trip to Central Park to see the turning leaves. She needed color. And those leaves would be gone after tonight's freeze.

Her belly began to burn. She had finally been diagnosed with obstetric cholestasis. Something to do with hormones and her liver, causing bile acids to be higher than normal in her blood stream. Her obstetrician prescribed medicine, which she took three times a day, but she also used Leoni's cream to ease the discomfort.

There were risks for the baby. Preterm birth. Heart and lung complications. Still birth.

Pete said "bad baby." Could he sense that something was wrong? She read somewhere that many animals had a sixth sense, a sort of intuition about cancers, epilepsy, and other illnesses. But she had never heard of this coming from a bird. She shook her head. She would not think those things.

The cushions on her outdoor glider made a soft whoosh as she sat down. The sounds of the city, thirty stories below her, rose around in muted noise. Car horns, busses and taxis, people talking and laughing, life moving by as if she didn't exist. Music from a passing car, the bass booming so loud she could feel it pounding in her chest. Even at this height.

Someone was playing a guitar. The song was slow and soothing. It took her a moment to realize that the sound was not coming from the street below, but from the terrace next door. It was the same music he was playing from his sound system during dinner that first night. She laid her head back against the seat and let the notes wash over her. Her baby would be fine.

CHAPTER FOURTEEN

David entered his office, tired from a weekend of no sleep. He blamed the full moon, and something about a lunar eclipse, which he couldn't see but social media had pictures of from around the world. He scrolled through his phone during the ride to the office, and Carlos, his driver, enthusiastically described his own view of the event, which occurred in the wee hours of the morning. A picture stared back at him. The face on the man in the moon was angry, the red glow from the eclipse glaring at him as if he had caused all the woes in the world.

He hadn't. Had he?

He had watched Elizabeth from his terrace as she sat with her head back, her hand over her swelling stomach. That was his baby. His son, growing in her womb. And he denied his part in her pregnancy.

He didn't know how Nathan learned the gender, but the man was a valuable source of information.

He would be a father in a little over three months. Just after the new year. He could deny it all he wanted to, but it wouldn't change the facts. What would she name the child? Would she call him David? Or Edward, his middle name? If she did, it would confirm to the world what many already suspected.

He listened to his favorite music, trying to calm the anxiousness growing within him, but it hadn't helped. He put a fist to his stomach as bile rose to his throat. The burning pain slid slowly down, mocking him.

"William, do you have any antacids?"

His assistant responded by bringing a large bottle into his office.

"Are you okay, sir? Do I need to call a doctor? You are at the prime age for a heart attack. I hear it feels a lot like indigestion."

David frowned at his assistant. His very astute, capable, assistant. William was closer to Elizabeth's age and would make some lucky lady a great husband someday. He would dote on her and never miss a detail. David deepened his frown.

"No, William. Just leave the bottle, please."

"Yes, sir. Let me know if you need anything else." His assistant gave him a concerned look before leaving the room.

Turning back to his work, he checked his emails and responded where needed. He had to sleep tonight. An over the counter sleeping medicine might help, but he didn't want to ask for that, too. For now, he focused on getting through this day.

———

Nathan entered an hour later for their scheduled meeting.

"What's wrong?" The attorney studied his face.

"Just some indigestion. That's all." He dismissed the question with a wave of his hand.

"Sympathetic pains?" Nathan sat down in the chair across the desk from David and crossed his ankle over the other knee. It was his standard casual pose.

"What are you talking about?"

"When my wife was pregnant with our daughter, she had indigestion. And I felt every pain. The doctor called it sympathetic pains."

"I haven't seen Elizabeth in months. I have no idea how . . ." He paused, suddenly realizing he had confirmed Nathan's suspicions. He mumbled as he finished the sentence. ". . . how she is feeling."

"I bet she is having heartburn, too." Nathan's tone was soft.

"I wouldn't know." He tried to back-track.

"Well, there is one way to find out."

"Aren't you here to discuss the Jordan deal?" He was getting irritated.

The attorney smirked. "Why don't you make this right? Just call her, David."

"Look, it was a mistake from the start. A small blip on the stupid meter. She taunted me from her rooftop. I fell for it. End of story.

"I thought you sent an invitation."

"That's confidential. The only person who knew that is William." David flipped his hair off his forehead. He needed a haircut.

Nathan sighed. "He has your best interest at heart. And you know, I'm a good attorney. I can get blood from a turnip. Or a confession from the most stubborn man." He cocked an eyebrow.

David leaned his head back and rubbed his hand over his chin.

"What should I do, Nathan?" He finally caved.

"You know what you need to do."

———

The charity event was swimming with donors. The host was raising money for an organization that supported abused women. Elizabeth liked this charity because the CEO received only a token salary. So many other nonprofits had highly paid executives in charge, and very little of the donated funds went to support the particular need. This one was different.

Elizabeth worked the room, greeting and meeting as she strolled between the tables. Leoni's new design drew attention from both men and women. The dress hung in gentle folds, its muted colors of grays and browns hiding her protruding abdomen. A pop of bright red trim on the bodice kept the eyes on top. Her swollen bosom certainly helped there, as did her makeup. Leoni had recommended the stylist, and Elizabeth loved the exotic look.

As she neared the host's table, her eyes locked with the man who invaded her thoughts several times a day. Of course David would be here, and he was likely a major donor. You didn't get a seat at the host's table by giving modest amounts. Donors at this table gave millions.

Her hand automatically went to her stomach. It was a gut reaction, but it drew his eyes to her middle. Her skin burned, the fiery pain spreading across her belly. She immediately moved her hand to her neck to keep from rubbing and caressed the diamond necklace on loan from a famous jewelry store. He turned his attention to the man next to him, who asked him a question, and she moved on to the next table.

Her escort for the night was an up-and-coming actor. Leoni knew him through other contacts and suggested she bring him with her. Tall, suave, and eye-popping gorgeous. Other women threw glares at her as he escorted her around the room. But there was no relationship. No spark, no attraction between them. He was just a man, paid to act as her date for this exclusive event.

Elizabeth couldn't even remember his name. He wrapped his arm around her shoulders and leaned down to speak into her ear.

"Everything okay?"

He was tempting to look at, but he was using her to get his name out, the same as she was using him as a plus-one for the event. He looked at David, then at Elizabeth, concern making a crease between his eyes.

"I'm fine. Just a touch of indigestion."

"Would you like some water?" He straightened slightly, his hand still on her shoulder. It was almost a caress as it slid across her back. He played his part well.

"Yes, please, and some crackers?" Sending her escort on the errand, she glanced back at David one more time. His eyes bore into hers, and she felt the heat from across the room. Swallowing her last bite, she made her decision. She didn't want to be here where David could stare at her. She had made her appearance, and done her job. It was time to go home.

———

David stared, unable to pull his eyes away from the vixen who haunted him day and night. There had to be a solution to their dilemma, but for the first time in his life, he didn't know what to do. Nathan hadn't been much help, urging him to call Elizabeth and "make things right," as he called it.

He didn't recognize the man with her. He was young and manicured and drooling over her. David frowned when the actor leaned into her ear, likely suggesting they slip away together. He smiled inwardly when she sent the man away. His host tapped him on his arm and pointed toward Elizabeth.

"She's a beauty, isn't she?"

"No argument there." He took a sip of his champagne.

"Too bad her husband didn't live long enough to see his child."

David almost choked on the bubbles. "Yuri was a great loss."

"That's right. He worked for you, didn't he?"

"He was my vice president of foreign acquisitions." He focused on his host.

"I remember the story. You lost several people that day."

"Yes. It was tragic. But we eventually got the deal, so their deaths were not in vain. Still, it was a high cost." His eyes turned back to Elizabeth.

"Well, it looks like she has landed on her feet."

"I hear she is doing well." Her young escort returned with crackers. She said something to him, and he placed his hand on her back, guiding her to the exit.

They were leaving?

Chapter Fifteen

Two more weeks passed. Elizabeth and Leoni were attending a Broadway show. Leoni's new designs were gathering attention, and Elizabeth was receiving more invitations than she could have ever imagined. This latest invite was from a Broadway producer who Leoni was courting as a potential costuming client. The show was a new, contemporary version of one done almost a hundred years ago about a showboat cruising up and down the Mississippi River. The crowd surrounding them in the orchestra section included the very rich and famous. Leoni scored a couple of prized seats for them, and Elizabeth was showing off another new gown.

When intermission was announced, they walked through the crowd to the elaborate lobby, which was decorated in the style of the Roaring Twenties. Elizabeth's gown was long but had the look of the flapper, beads swinging with each step she took. The silky material shimmered like water under the beads. Her short wig and makeup made her feel straight out of the era, and the beaded band and feathers completed the look.

A man bumped into her, and she felt a twinge in her stomach. Bending over, she realized the sensation was not from the man's bump, but from the baby within. She grabbed Leoni's elbow for balance.

"Let's go to the ladies' room."

"Are you alright?"

Elizabeth bent as she received another kick. "The baby wants attention."

They quickly strode to a lounge area where she hoped they would have some privacy. Her hand instinctively rested on her stomach, and she couldn't stop the mixed look of joy and panic on her face.

"How far along are you?" Leoni kept her voice low.

"Twenty-seven weeks. Here." Elizabeth moved to a cushioned bench. "Let's sit here." She gasped as the baby kicked again and looked around quickly. There was no one else in the room. She took Leoni's hand and laid it over her stomach, on her left side just under her rib.

"There. Feel that? He kicked again." Her skin burned with the assault from her womb.

Leoni smiled. "This is life. Beautiful, beautiful life. And he will be a strong one, for sure." Leoni winked, and they laughed together.

"Have you decided on a name, yet?"

Elizabeth froze, her mouth turned down in a frown. "No."

"Why not?"

"If I give him the name I want to, it will give away his identity. If I name him after Yuri, well, that wouldn't be right, either." She felt the bump to her hand as the foot pushed against her abdomen and was suddenly overwhelmed. A tear slid down her face.

"Oh, Leoni. What am I going to do?"

Leoni took her hands and grabbed her focus with her eyes. "Listen, honey. This child is a gift from God. He may not approve of the way the baby was conceived, but He still has a plan for him, and for you. I don't know what that plan is, but I'm here for you." The designer squeezed her hands.

"I have no one, Leoni." Elizabeth couldn't stop the flow of tears. She knew her makeup would be a mess. "No father for my baby. Real or otherwise. No one who really cares about me, other than my grandfather. And he can't take care of me, nor should he have to."

"Is your grandfather nearby?"

Elizabeth shook her head. Her relationship to Antoni wasn't common knowledge. In fact, only a small handful of people knew she was his heir, and she wanted to keep it that way. Leoni wrapped her arms around Elizabeth, and their perfumes mingled as the two sat in silence.

"There. There, he kicked again." She drew in a quick breath.

The lights blinked as intermission ended. Orchestral music filled the lobby, reminding visitors it was time for the next act. The crowd made their way back to their seats, but Elizabeth and Leoni sat in the alcove, the play forgotten as her designer and friend provided the motherly comfort that she lacked.

Elizabeth laughed. "I think I need some chocolate. But first, I need to relieve myself. This little football player is sitting on my bladder."

Leoni squeezed her hand one more time. "Follow me." But they looked up, startled, as the last person Elizabeth expected to see walked around the corner toward them.

———

The crowd swarmed during intermission, jostling David as he made his way to the men's room. He had seen Elizabeth and Leoni from his box seat and wondered if he would run into her, preferring to not be seen. A man bumped into him, and he stepped aside, but as he did, he saw the same man bump into Elizabeth. He quickly checked his pockets to make sure he had not just been a victim of a thief, but his wallet was still in place. When he looked up again, she had disappeared.

He made his way to the lounge area, took care of his business, and headed down the purple and blue hallway when voices caught his attention. They were coming from a connecting rose-and-gold hallway. He realized he was adjacent to the women's lounge.

". . . he kicked again."

The baby was kicking? He stopped in his tracks. What would it feel like to have a child growing inside his body? The surreal knowledge that you were an incubator for another soul? His curiosity grew, and he stepped closer, wanting to hear more but careful to stay out of sight.

He had read several articles on childbirth, wanting to understand anything that could affect the child. Even though he wasn't ready to acknowledge the baby as his, he still wanted to be ready for anything that could happen.

The first flutter. He had already missed that.

The first kick. Was that tonight?

The first imprint of the tiny foot as he pushed against Elizabeth's stomach.

The first breath.

The first cry.

The first time those beautiful baby's eyes would look into his face with undeserved love.

"I have no one, Leoni."

David startled at her words. How would she handle being a single mother? He had no idea how to raise a child and wasn't sure what she would need. Diapers? Three a.m. feedings? Would she breastfeed or use a bottle? Would the baby even take one or the other?

And what would happen through the years? Would Elizabeth find someone to love and care for her and the boy, or would she stay alone forever? The thoughts unsettled him.

He had to see her. This was his chance. The alcove was isolated, and no one walked in and out while he stood there listening. He took a deep breath and stepped out of the connecting gray hallway into the one leading to the ladies' lounge. Elizabeth and Leoni were sitting on a bench just a few feet away, with Leoni's hand on Elizabeth's growing abdomen. He cleared his throat, and Elizabeth looked up, startled.

"David." The word was sharper than his entire sword collection, her jasmine perfume punctuating his feelings.

"Hello, Elizabeth." He stood still as a rock, while inside he quivered from head to toe. His CEO instincts told him this wasn't a good idea.

"What are you doing here?"

"I heard you talking and wanted to check on you. Are you okay?"

She frowned at him. "Yes, David. I'm fine."

"You sounded like you were in distress. Upset." He walked closer to them. Leoni gave him a curious look.

"I'm just tired. The baby is kicking." She paused before giving him a side-eye. "Why do you care now?" That last word said everything she wanted him to know.

"I've been worried about you. You know, since Yuri died.

He looked at his feet, his hands on his hips, then back up to her eyes. "If you need to leave, I would be happy to call a cab for you."

She stared at him without responding. She seemed frozen in thought.

"Or, better yet, I will call my car for you. Carlos can take you home." He laid a soft hand on her shoulder and felt her stiffen. But he refused to remove his hand, choosing instead to rub his thumb on the tender spot between her neck and shoulder.

Leoni looked back and forth between them. "I should give you two some privacy." She moved to stand.

"No." Elizabeth caught Leoni's arm. "Don't leave." Leoni sat back down.

David was secretly relieved Elizabeth had such a good friend. But then she slapped his hand away from her shoulder and stood abruptly, forcing him to take a step backwards. Her words spilled from her mouth. She couldn't have made it more clear. Or icy.

"I don't need a cab. I don't need your car or your driver. I don't need your money or your stupid trust fund. Or you. My son and I will be just fine." She took a short breath, barely stopping. "But I do need chocolate. And peanut butter. And a dill pickle. And a bathroom." She speared him with her eyes. She meant business.

"Come on, Leoni."

Her friend and designer chuckled as David watched them enter the ladies' room. Leoni gave him a look that said he was the worst kind of cad. Was he?

"He's the father?"

Elizabeth's simple nod was her only acknowledgement as they started around the corner, out of sight. This could get sticky. He would have to check in with Nathan to make sure Elizabeth had every available resource, whether she wanted it or not. But she said she didn't need him. That was what stung the worst. Even if he wouldn't acknowledge the baby.

———

"What's up, David?" His attorney and friend looked up as David walked into his office, going straight to the window to look out from the forty-third floor. It was mid-October, but there was no sign of Autumn in Manhattan unless he made the five-mile trek to Central Park. The leaves had probably already reached their peak colors there. He had missed it all.

Nathan waited as he looked out the window. Turning away from the view, he walked to the chair across from the desk and slumped into the leather.

"I went to see a show last night."

"And that made you look like your last cat died?" Nathan tapped a few keys on his laptop and closed the lid.

"I saw Elizabeth there."

"Ah. That explains it all." Nathan gave him a compassionate look. The man was a saint.

"Did you feel your daughter when she kicked?" He rested his elbow on the arm of the chair and sat up slightly.

Nathan laughed. "No, my wife felt every kick, I promise."

"No. What I mean is, did you have a chance to feel it with her?" He looked away briefly before turning his eyes back.

Nathan leveled his gaze, making David uncomfortable. "What brought this on?"

He fidgeted, which was something he never did. "I saw her during intermission, talking to Leoni about the baby kicking. They were giggling at first, then she started crying."

"You talked to her?" Nathan's eyes grew wide. He knew David's challenges and risks.

"I heard them talking from an adjoining hallway."

"So, you were spying on her." His friend knew him too well.

He stared back at his friend. He wouldn't admit he did actually talk to her.

"Come on, David. Confess. You talked to her."

He sighed. "Yes, and Leoni was with her."

"I see. So now she knows, too." Nathan crossed his arms over his chest. "But I still don't understand. You won't even acknowledge the baby. Why?"

David shrugged, looking at the picture of Nathan's family on the bookshelf.

"You're missing out on something wonderful." Nathan lowered his gaze knowingly.

"It's crossed my mind." He turned his head to look over Nathan's shoulder at the view outside his window. A ship was cruising up the harbor.

"You can still make it right."

"No, Nathan. It is much too late for that."

"Look. You are David Kingston. You own an empire. You have resources, people bowing at your feet to do whatever you ask. If I were in your shoes, I would be moving heaven and earth to be as close as possible to my son. Whether you and Elizabeth are together or not." Nathan opened his desk drawer, pulled out a stress ball, and tossed it at David."

Reaching up without thinking, David caught the ball in his fingers and tossed it back.

"I don't want to take the baby away from her. Can you see me as a single dad? I would have to hire a nanny, and the poor kid would spend more time with her than with me. Besides, you know what kind of fallout there would be."

He caught the ball as Nathan tossed it back again. They had done this often when they were first starting out. The exercise helped them to focus on an issue without distraction, filtering out any other concerns that might be getting in the way of their discussion. It soothed his worries. The simple red rubber sphere flew back and forth several times before he stood. He tossed it back to Nathan one last time and walked back to the window. The sky was getting cloudy, and he could see his reflection in the specially tempered glass. It was supposed to withstand hurricane-force winds. But there was a hurricane swirling around him as he stood there that the glass could not stop.

Who was he? Who did he see in his reflection? He was a highly powerful man. His blue eyes shone with brilliance and shrewd intelligence. His Italian silk suit was specially tailored to fit over his strong sculptured frame, as if DaVinci himself had designed it. His muscles rippled under the expensive couture, confidence exuding from his posture. It was a practiced stance, meant to send a message to anyone he encountered.

Nathan said he should make it right with Elizabeth. What did that even look like? He tried to make a settlement. What more did she want? Should he claim the child? No. Yes. No. He had never been this confused on any issue.

The red ball smacked him in the side of the head, knocking him out of his brooding. He turned sharply to Nathan.

"What?"

Nathan looked over the glasses that sat on his nose. "David."

David sighed as he turned more fully. "What, Nathan? I'm out of answers."

Nathan slid his readers off his face. "I'm your attorney. You pay me very nicely to give you solid advice. And to be frank with you. So this is how I see things."

David nodded for Nathan to continue.

"Legally, you don't have to do anything."

Nathan paused, and David waited.

"Financially, you have already offered a settlement. She hasn't accepted it. That's her choice."

"This is nothing new, Nathan." David put his hands on his hips.

"Emotionally? You know how women are. They want love and stability. Seems to me that Elizabeth has neither right now."

"I don't have enough love left to share with any woman. I've been there, done that. Twice. It didn't work out either time."

Nathan ignored his response and kept right on going, locking eyes with David with finality.

"And morally? Well, only you and God can answer that question."

Chapter Sixteen

ELIZABETH HELD onto the corner of the wall until the dizzy wave passed. She hadn't been feeling well for several days. Nothing extreme. Just indigestion, mostly. At almost eight months pregnant, she wasn't sure what to expect, but she didn't think this was normal. She had lived on antacid tablets for the past several months but hadn't experienced the lightheadedness she was feeling now. She paused, waiting until her head cleared before she continued her path across the room to her kitchen. A glass of water might help.

A cramp seared through her as she reached the island that separated the kitchen from the living space. This wasn't a contraction, was it? It was too soon for Braxton Hicks. Grabbing her stomach, she bent over, clutching the counter with her other hand.

"Oooooh!" The cry tore from her throat without thought. She panted through the pain. A piercing squawk came from the bird cage in response.

"God help me." A whisper was all she could muster. A warm feeling leaked down her leg.

Another cramp. This one was more severe. She bent deeply, closing her eyes and gasping through the pain, and dragged her hand over the counter for support. Collapsing to the floor, her phone fell beside her. She blindly patted the cold marble tile until she found it lying in a puddle of warm liquid.

Dizzy. She was so dizzy. And was that blood or water between her legs? It was too soon. Too soon. Panic swept through her, and she tried to open her eyes as the pain continued to flash across her belly like a lightning strike. Unable to move, she picked up her phone with shaking hands and hit redial. She had no idea who her last call had been to but was glad when a male voice answered the call. Was it David? Her head spun as she tried to recognize the voice.

"Baby. Too soon. Help me."

A loud squawk filled the air. "Too soon. Too soon."

She dropped the phone as everything went black.

———

Nathan knocked on David's door and entered without waiting.

"Elizabeth called a few minutes ago. I believe the baby is in trouble."

"What happened?" David looked up from another cost analysis spreadsheet.

"The phone rang, and I saw her number. I just called her yesterday to remind her about the trust paperwork. All I heard today was 'Baby. Too soon.' Then she collapsed. I think she passed out. So I called 911 for her. I don't know why she called me instead of them."

"Is she at home?" He tapped his forefinger on his desk. His heart began to pound. Elizabeth was in trouble. His son was in trouble. But he was frozen, afraid to move. Afraid of his emotions and the cost. He pushed his hair out of his face, running his fingers over his head to the back of his neck.

"I think so. There was a loud shriek right before the call died but it sounded like a bird."

"She has a macaw."

"Okay. Well, then I sent the ambulance to the right place. Do you know the code to her apartment?" Nathan was the voice of calm.

"No. I've never been over there."

"You own the building. I'll call the building manager and put him on alert. He can make sure EMS gets in."

"Thank you. Keep me informed." He turned back to his spreadsheet, numb.

"Aren't you going to the hospital? I would be the first one out the door right now if I were you. You should be rushing to be there. What if she dies?" Nathan gave him a look that David had never seen from him before. Was that contempt? He looked away, unwilling to bear his friend's judgment.

"I doubt she wants me there. Besides, I can't risk the connection right now."

Nathan shook his head, his eyes narrowed as he scoffed. "Of course you can't. Whatever you do, don't compromise your reputation as the house that God built."

David pointed at Nathan, irked at the man's righteous remark. "If you weren't my friend, I would fire you. In fact, I might still do that."

"You can't afford it." They locked eyes. David knew his attorney wasn't talking about money.

"Go to the hospital. Find out what she needs. And keep me informed." He waved his hand, the invitation to leave clear. He needed to think. Nathan walked out and quietly closed the door behind him.

David sighed and leaned back in his chair, closing his eyes.

The baby was in trouble. David counted silently from last spring. It was November now, almost Thanksgiving. Not quite thirty-three weeks, if she got pregnant the first night. Almost two months early.

He straightened and started researching preemie deliveries on his laptop. There were too many complications listed. Too many things to go wrong.

Low birth weight. Underdeveloped lungs. Hole in the heart.

Cerebral palsy. Impaired learning, vision, hearing. The list went on and on for the baby.

For the mother, there was risk of seizures, cardiovascular disease, blood clots, damage to liver or kidneys.

David felt ill. This was all his fault. He sent a message to Nathan.

"Don't let her die, Nathan. Make sure she has the best medical team available. I want the best of the best. No matter the cost. I can't have another death on my hands."

It all boiled down to money and reputation, and it was selfish. He had tried to buy Elizabeth off, and she turned him down. The money sat in the trust funds, untouched. But hospitals were usually first in line for any kind of monetary donation. His foundation could make the gift anonymously. It had been long enough since the fiasco with the reporter that everyone had surely forgotten.

A week went by. The hospital would not give anyone an update on Elizabeth's status, not even Nathan. David paced his office. Even his money could not buy his way through the HIPAA privacy laws. Didn't being guarantor on her doctor bills apply to the hospital? Apparently not. He watched the street below from his Ivory Palace, as Nathan called it, and prayed. And as much as he wanted to be a man after God's own heart, he couldn't bring himself to pray "Thy will be done." It was more like "God, please do something."

———

The doctor held Elizabeth's hand as he delivered the news.

"We've delayed the birth as long as possible. We've given you supplements to strengthen his lungs and heart, but your body is rebelling. Blood pressure is high, white cell count is starting to rise. We need to take the baby."

"What will that mean? How will you do that? And will he live? I don't really care about myself."

Patting her hand, he put his stethoscope into his ears and listened to all her vitals again. Her own heart and lungs. Sounds from the large mound of flesh she called her stomach. No, not just flesh. A living, breathing baby boy, struggling for life.

"Let's try inducing. I'll get a team in here right away to start the process. Do you want an epidural?"

She had read up on the pain fighting procedure. A catheter would be inserted into a space near her spine, numbing her from the waist down so that she wouldn't feel the pain. If necessary, she could receive a second dose through the existing catheter, but that was rare. Most women received epidurals and had successful deliveries with only one dose.

"Will the pain medicine hurt the baby?"

"We need to reduce the stress on your body as much as possible. It will be easier on him, as well, given the circumstances." He patted her stomach.

Nodding, she agreed. "Okay. Let's do that, then."

"Great. We'll do that first, then start the Pitocin, which will cause you to go into labor. You'll need to sign for both. Also, is there anyone we can call for you? Most women have someone in attendance for their birth, but I know your husband is deceased. Do you have a friend who could come?" His look was compassionate, yet curious.

"No. Let's not bother anybody." Leoni had a show coming up. She wouldn't call her friend. And she couldn't call David. She could do this. She would do this.

———

The birth was anything but normal. The epidural didn't work. Not after the first dose. Not after the second dose. Nor the third dose. Had they done something wrong? Why wouldn't the pain stop? She wanted to call Leoni, but she was progressing so rapidly, she thought the baby would be born before Leoni arrived, anyway.

A nurse brought nitrous oxide at the doctor's request. She knew it was laughing gas. But it was self-administered. She was responsible for taking a deep breath from the mask whenever she felt the need.

A funny thought entered her head, and she giggled, feeling like she was floating above the scene. But it did not reduce the pain. It just gave her a feeling of indifference. She laid back and waited for the next contraction, wishing she had someone here to hold her hand.

They began coming in rapid succession. She had already been in labor for nearly five hours, and now she was barely able to catch her breath from one before the next one came. Each pain was stronger than the last, with no time between to take another breath. Her laughing gas was forgotten. Her body was being ravaged from the inside. She feared she would never be the same again.

"Oh, God. Oh, God. Help me. Help me. Help me." Was that a prayer or a curse? She didn't care.

"God, please stop the pain." The prayer tore from her throat. Her eyes wide, she worried that she was dying. She couldn't stop the tears from rolling down her face. What would heaven look like? Would Yuri be there to meet her? Or would he sneer at her as she succumbed from delivering another man's baby?

"I don't have the strength." She couldn't even get her breath between pains.

"Yes, you do, darling. You can do this. You're almost there."

A nurse stood on either side of her, supporting her as they lifted her back to sit up and her knees to her chest to help her push. She roared as she squeezed.

"Get this thing out of me!"

"Just a couple more pushes. I see curly hair. His little head is right there."

She pushed again, and suddenly she felt relief, but the next pain came almost immediately, and she knew this was it. The doctor and nurses quickly surrounded the baby as he slid from her womb. Collapsing onto the bed, she closed her eyes, waiting to hear his cry. But it didn't come.

"What's wrong?" She tried to rise. "My baby. Where is my baby? Is he okay?"

A nurse was immediately at her side. "He's being taken to the

NICU. The Neonatal Intensive Care Unit. That is normal protocol for early births like yours." The nurse patted her hand.

"Is he okay? I want to see him."

"He was not breathing at first, but we were able to revive him. You have a beautiful baby boy."

"Not breathing? What's wrong with him?" She asked the questions, looking frantically from side to side while another nurse began stitching her up. The delivery had, indeed, torn her body.

"He's just small. We see this a lot with preemies. Don't worry. He will get the best of care." The compassion in the nurse's eyes brought on another round of tears.

"I want my baby."

Tears streamed down her face, her emotions taking over. Eyes closed, she allowed the despair to cover her.

Chapter Seventeen

The next day, David looked up from his laptop as Nathan walked into his office unannounced. He had been trying to focus on numbers from the latest review.

"She had the baby. It's a boy, but I guess you knew that. He is in the NICU, fighting for his life. If you want to see him, you need to get to the hospital. I have made arrangements for you."

A son. He had a son.

His heart felt full and empty at the same time. Only Nathan and Elizabeth knew he was the father. But he had built a series of lies and deceptions designed to deny the relationship. Now he had a son that he couldn't acknowledge.

"'Oh what a tangled web we weave, when first we practice to deceive.'" He recalled the phrase from a poem by Sir Walter Scott. Literature hadn't been his best subject, but a couple of quotes had stuck with him through the years.

"I'm sorry. What did you say?" Nathan looked at him with a frown.

"'O wad some Power the giftie gie us, to see oursels as ithers see us!'" Robert Burns had it right. He was a louse. A stinky, filthy rat trying to hide in plain site on a beautiful lady's bonnet. Unfortunately, he was on display for all the world to see. Or he would be, if this hit the media. Still, he had to go. He had to know.

Later that day, David entered the NICU, tiptoeing quietly to avoid disturbing the babies. He waited until the end of visiting hours to avoid running into anyone who might identify him. A nurse stopped him, making him sign in, and checked to see that he was on the approved visitor list. He was surprised to find that he was. She took his temperature to make sure he wasn't carrying in any illness. Handing him a yellow paper robe, she helped him put it on backwards and tie it behind his neck. She showed him where to scrub up, then handed him a paper cap, gloves, and a mask.

He felt like a surgeon.

He wasn't listed as the father. But he had offered a donation to the unit in order to see the baby. Money always talked louder than anything else. But somehow, his name was on the approved visitor list.

As they entered the NICU, the antiseptic smell of alcohol and other cleaners assaulted his nose. He knew they had to keep this environment as germ-free as possible for the sake of the little ones. Most were born premature. Some were as many as two or even three months early. He passed by an enclosed crib called an incubator that held a baby smaller than some of the dolls he had once seen in a discount store back in Iowa. He said a silent prayer for the little girl and her parents.

The nurse led him to a row of enclosed beds near the back of the unit. Monitoring screens stood sentry over each bed, listing vital stats including heart rate and oxygen saturation. A mobile computer station held a swinging keyboard and could be rolled to each bed as the doctors and nurses made the rounds. Another nurse sat at the station, adding the click of the keyboard to the beeps surrounding them. David nodded silently to her.

A baby cried from a neighboring room that was set aside for isolation. It was a lonely, desolate sound of pain. David wondered how any of the nurses and technicians could work day after day in this environment. How could they watch the smallest of the small struggle to hang on to their very lives by a thread. How could they go home at the end of their shifts and sleep a sound sleep with pleasant dreams instead of nightmares? How could they coo so softly with love and compassion as they changed tiny diapers and swaddling? Inspected feeding tubes? Stuck their tiny feet with even tinier needles to draw the necessary blood samples? Rubbed their sensitive skin with cleansers and lotions? The sights and sounds surrounded him, pricking his brain. His own son was one of these babies. He wanted to turn and leave. He wanted to run.

Instead, he followed the nurse to a far corner, trying to stay focused on the task at hand. They stopped at a heated bed labeled "Baby Boy Yassin." Elizabeth's baby. Interesting. She had not yet given the baby a name.

He looked through the clear acrylic lid at the child that was not swaddled, as he had expected, but under a special light that the nurse explained was used to treat jaundice. Small cotton patches covered the baby's eyes, and a tiny tube was inserted through his nose. It would drip a special formula into his stomach. A sensor of some kind was taped to his foot, and a cord led back to his monitor. A tiny diaper with a puppy on the front was the only other thing he wore.

"May I hold him?" David hoped his request would be granted without having to explain why. The nurse looked at him, paused as if in thought, then nodded.

"I'll need to swaddle him first. Give me a moment."

She changed the diaper and wrapped the baby tightly in two blankets. Then she pulled a small, knitted hat over the child's wavy brown hair. Finally she took him out of the incubator and turned, pointing to a wooden rocker.

"Sit here, and I will hand the baby to you."

David sat as instructed and held out his arms to receive the baby. The child was small and felt like he weighed nothing at all. His large hands practically engulfed the baby. He stared at his son and swallowed, overwhelmed.

"May I see his eyes?" He looked up at the nurse. A tear hung in the corner of one eye, and he blinked it away.

"I can give you just a couple of minutes." The nurse regarded him for a moment before gently removing the patches.

Blue eyes stared at him. The color of the sky on a clear fall day. These were not the kind of eyes that would later turn brown. No. These were his own eyes staring back at him, fringed in lashes so thick and long, they could have been feathers. Women paid for expensive procedures to have lashes like this.

David ran a finger lightly over the baby's soft cheek and took in the shape of his nose. His chin was gently rounded with a small dimple in the center, his ears sitting close to his scalp. David lifted the cap to look again at the brown wavy hair and hairline, which mimicked his own.

He was holding his son. There was no denying it. They were a carbon copy of each other, all the way down to the small birthmark behind his left ear. He pulled his phone from under his own paper gown, snapped a quick picture, and tucked the phone away.

Looking up, he saw the nurse staring at him, recognition on her face. He had to say something.

"I assume you are familiar with HIPAA compliance laws?"

The nurse simply nodded.

"Then this will go no farther than this room. Correct?" He raised one eyebrow in a look that said he expected nothing less. The nurse nodded again, more slowly the second time.

He held the baby for a couple more minutes, kissing the babe's small cheek through his mask. Closing his eyes, he tried in vain to hide the tears building there.

"Thank you for your time." He handed the tiny infant back to the nurse, then stood to leave, a drop rolling down his face.

"Mr. Kingston?" The nurse found her voice.

He turned back to her.

"I will pray for your son. And for you."

David nodded in return, then went to the outer room where he removed the paper garments before slipping out the door. He left the NICU just as Antoni was entering.

"Antoni. What are you doing here?"

His friend and mentor looked at him knowingly. "I could ask you the same thing."

"The wife of one of my best employees just had her baby. Too early. I came to check on the child."

Antoni nodded. "Have you been to see Elizabeth?"

"No, I haven't wanted to bother her." How did the man know who he was talking about? He realized he made a slip with his response.

A code sounded over the hospital intercom speakers. It was the kind of code that said someone was in serious trouble. David listened to the announcement, then realized Antoni hadn't answered his question.

"Why are you here, Antoni?"

The man he had known for nearly two decades narrowed his eyes. "I know the baby is yours."

David coughed. "Excuse me?"

"I ran a DNA test on you."

David shifted but kept his cool. "Aside from the fact that that is completely illegal, what difference does it make to you? And how did you even do that?" He stepped closer to Antoni. Face to face. "Should I have a little talk with Nathan about this?"

"You drank coffee in my office. Remember? We got a DNA sample from that, and it was enough to run a test. It won't be submissible, of course. The courts only want a cheek swab. But we can get a subpoena for that." Antoni challenged David with his eyes.

"I ask again. Why is this your concern?" He crossed his arms and stared at his friend, one eyebrow quirked. It was a look that usually made men quickly acquiesce.

"Liza is my granddaughter." Antoni's smile was smug.

David wracked his brain, the sudden realization coming down on him like a sledgehammer on a steel spike. There it was. The thing on the tip of his tongue. The missing card in the deck. And the name his mind had been searching for.

Liza. Elizabeth. David nearly choked.

"The picture in your office of you and a little girl. That was Elizabeth. Why didn't anyone tell me about your relationship?"

"Liza wanted to keep it quiet. Yuri was working his way up through the company, and he didn't want anyone to be able to claim nepotism."

David paced away, then back, rubbing the back of his head. A lullaby played over the speakers. Another baby was just born. He pulled his mind away from the distraction.

Resigned to the inevitable, he nodded his head. "What has she told you?"

Antoni smirked. "Everything."

Somehow, David didn't think that was entirely true. The man was fishing for more. An older couple stepped off the elevator and headed their way, their faces a mixture of happiness and concern as they shuffled together toward the NICU. He stepped to the side to give them plenty of room, but also to make sure the couple could not overhear the conversation.

"I don't think this is the time or place, Antoni. Save it for later." He started toward the elevator.

"We will discuss this, David. You cannot escape your responsibility." Antoni called from behind him, his tone sharp. David knew there would be a price, but he couldn't imagine what that would be.

Disgruntled, he punched the button several times to call the elevator, wishing he had a private entrance. This was a new wrinkle that he needed to investigate further.

Chapter Eighteen

Elizabeth watched her son struggle to breathe as she rocked him in the chair assigned to her in the NICU. Tears slipped down her face. They had given her a private room for this moment. The doctors said he was very weak and recommended that he know he was loved in his final hours. They had done everything possible. But seven days after his birth, he was not improving. His life was slowly slipping away.

She was discharged the day after he was born. Her body had healed quickly. Blood pressure and white cell count were normal. The burning redness of her skin cleared up overnight. But she would trade anything, take all that pain back, if it would ensure that he would live.

Elizabeth was Israeli. According to Jewish custom going back thousands of years, baby boys were circumcised on the eighth day after their birth and the child named at that time. It was a ceremony called a *brit milah*, and though she was not a practicing Jew, she had planned to hold on to that tradition.

Now she held him in her arms for what might be the last time. His tiny chest heaved with each breath, his abdomen sucking in and out, the effort slowing with each passing moment. He looked up at her, his large blue eyes filled with love and pain, begging her for help, and she tried not to cry. She had to be brave so that he would be brave.

Elizabeth lost track of time as she sat there, holding her son. She spent Thanksgiving Day at home alone before getting the call from the doctor early this morning. Now, Fifth Avenue was full of people out shopping for the hottest Christmas specials while she was holding her son as his life ebbed away. Her foot automatically pushed them back and forth in the rocker, the slow motion soothing. A nurse peeked into the room a couple of times, and Elizabeth smiled sadly. Then she was left in privacy again.

The intercom was shut off in the room. She didn't want to hear the lullaby play as each new baby was born while she was saying goodbye to her own. The silence surrounded them, the only sound the soft swish of the chair as it rocked. Even the sounds of the monitors were muted, although the nurses still received the feed at the nurses' station.

Needing to break the silence, she sang to him, a song she remembered from her days in church school. Her notes were off-key, but the message was clear.

"This little light of mine. I'm gonna let it shine."

She choked on the words as she sang them, over and over. The light in her son's eyes grew dim, the blue not quite as vibrant as it was seven days ago. But she stayed focused, willing him to keep fighting. To keep breathing. To keep shining his light.

Shadows moved across the floor, from one side of the rocker to the other, as the sun moved through the sky. The view from her window held the gray granite wall of the wing next door. The cancer ward. Children over there were struggling to live, too. Why would God bring such beautiful children into the world only to take them away, leaving behind grieving parents with no answers? She just didn't understand.

Was this punishment for her sin? Was this the consequence of throwing herself at a man she couldn't have? Or was this some weird quirk of fate, a lottery of sorts that decreed so many must die in order for others to live? If so, why take the babies?

She took a deep breath, shuddering as she exhaled. She needed to remain calm for her son. Pushing with her foot, she set the rocker into motion again.

Her eyes studied his face, committing it to memory in her heart. She gazed into his own beautiful eyes. So full of love. And so like his father's. Kissing his forehead, she ran her finger over his cheeks, pouring all the love she could muster into the action. Felt the feathery softness of his long, luscious lashes. Traced his tiny nose. Over his precious lips. Along the dimple in his chin. Around his ears, perfectly shaped for listening to quiet guitar music.

Picking up one hand, she urged his fingers to close around hers. And they did.

They sat in perfect union as the shadows moved again, the sky turning dark.

Then she felt it. One final stir as his hand fell away.

Looking down, she realized his chest was no longer moving. The gasp she heard was her own. His eyes had closed, and his face was peaceful. Now, the dam broke, and a flood poured from her own eyes as she hugged her son close to her chest. Maybe her heartbeat would be enough for both of them. Maybe he would breathe again.

But it was not to be.

The nurse peeked her head into the room. "Take all the time you need."

She nodded and continued to rock. She didn't know how long they would let her stay with him, to hold him, but she would take every precious minute with him that she could. She did not want to go home with empty arms.

———

Elizabeth entered her luxury penthouse suite hours later, walking through the dark room to the kitchen area on autopilot. The hospital called a cab for her, the nurses chipping in to pay for it out of their own pockets. They even ordered a takeout meal for her, but she wasn't in the mood to eat, so she set the small white cardboard tub on the dining table next to her phone.

"Hello." Pete shuffled in his cage. She had forgotten about him.

"Hello, Pete." She opened her refrigerator, pulled out a piece of fruit for him, and fed the bird through the bars of the cage.

"Baby with God?" How did this bird get so smart?

"Yes, Pete. Baby with God."

"I'm sorry." This was not a new phrase, but it still shook her.

"Thank you, Pete."

She zipped his cover and walked back into her living area, thinking to watch something on television to distract her mind, but she didn't want to watch a cutesy happy-ever-after movie, and sitcoms didn't appeal, either, so she found a late-night infomercial for cookware, left it on for a background, and muted the sound.

Slipping her shoes off, she set them to the side and stretched out on her sofa.

Quiet. The house was too quiet.

The beautiful baby she had held in her arms a few short hours ago was now resting peacefully in the arms of the Lord. Or at least, that was what one of the nurses had said. She wasn't sure how she felt about that. She wanted to believe in God, but right now her heart couldn't reconcile a loving God with the pain in her heart.

She had been terrified, then angry when she learned she was pregnant. But as the baby grew in her womb, she had become accustomed to his presence as a source of comfort. She had been looking forward to the days when she would change his first diaper.

Feed him his first baby food. Watch him splash in a bathtub full of toys. Scooting toy trucks around the floor with him. Picking up his first crayon. Taking the crayon from his mouth.

Pitching a ball with him, back and forth. Dressing him in cute little clothes and taking him with her to Leoni's shop for all her clients to see. Picking him up from school. Talking to him about girls. Helping him dress for his first date. Sending him off to college. Meeting the girl he would bring home with him and declare was "the one." Watching him stand next to the preacher as he waited for "the one" to walk down the aisle, ready to pledge her love and life to him.

Holding her first grandchild.

Now, those days were only a dream in her mind. A fantasy that hadn't come true.

She laid her arm over her eyes and slowly drifted off to sleep.

CHAPTER NINETEEN

DESPITE HOW THE news had gotten out, the fact remained that it had. Headlines were splashed across newspapers and tabloid TV shows. Late night comedians made fun of him, parody shows mocked him, and social media had several hashtags trending. #Kingstonbabydaddy. #NYCroyalaffair. #adulteryandmurder. His stock plunged.

The day after Thanksgiving, seven days after his birth, the baby died. Elizabeth hadn't even given the child a name. He was just Baby Boy Yassin. It gave a new meaning to Black Friday.

The world was shocked. The news suddenly shifted to other subjects, as if they all had something to do with the baby's death. But David's troubles had just begun.

He walked into his penthouse suite, frustrated. It was a difficult meeting with his board, where they demanded answers for the articles appearing not only in the nightly news but in the stock market news, as well. His indiscretions cost the company millions of dollars as investors pulled out. Never mind the fact that he knew many of those same investors were casting stones they had no right to cast. Still, the damage was done. Kingston Holdings, Incorporated was in serious trouble.

He didn't know who the whistleblower was. It was not Elizabeth. Or Antoni, which surprised him. Somebody in the hospital had seen him. Had seen the baby. Had seen the undeniable resemblance between them. If it was the nurse, he could easily make both her and the hospital pay for such a flagrant violation of privacy. But he had no proof of who had gone to the press. All he had was an "unnamed source." And the press wouldn't give up their secret informant.

Now his stock was tumbling. He still had other divisions, but the board said it was important to separate those divisions immediately from the parent company. James, the lecher from the gala, would head up the transportation division. Grayson, a known philanderer, would head up the energy division. But they hadn't sold themselves on being pure and upright. They weren't the giant among giants, as David was touted. No, they were setting themselves up to be the giant-killers.

Recalling the meeting, he felt the tension building in him again. How dare they?

"You have a morality clause, David. You have violated the clause." James took a casual sip of water, his eyes cool.

"And you know what they say about throwing stones when you live in a glass house. Gentlemen." David speared each of them with a look.

James. The perpetual skirt-chaser.

Grayson. Married with benefits on the side.

The senator. Who knew what side he was on?

Antoni. His friend. At least he used to be. Now David wasn't sure.

"Look, our lives aren't under the microscope." James set the glass down.

"My personal life is my business." David stood at one end of the table, his hands flattened on the shiny glass surface.

"Not when it is tied to the company like this. Not when it impacts all of us. Our investments in your company. And in you. When your stock tanks, financial or otherwise, ours tank with it."

"You are welcome to pull out."

"And take such a tremendous loss? I think not." James picked up his glass again and pointed it at David. "In fact, I think you should cash in your chips and go back to Hicksville. Or wherever you are from. We'll take over from here."

"Who is going to force me out?" David stood up straight and crossed his arms. He still had controlling interest. James stood, too, mimicking David's stance. Challenging.

Antoni stood between them. "David, you had an affair. With my granddaughter, no less."

"Which you failed to disclose." David turned abruptly toward his mentor.

"She wanted it that way. But then you killed her husband."

"I did not kill her husband!" He raised his voice. Yes, he sent the team to Jordan. But he had no idea they would be attacked so violently. He lowered his voice again.

"Others died that day, too. I am sorry for all of them." He sat back down, rubbing his face as he did.

"And now my grandson is dead, too." Antoni's words dripped with poison.

"For which I am very sorry. But I have no control over who lives and who dies. I'm not God, Antoni."

"You sure set yourself up that way. To the world out there." Antoni pointed out the window. "You own companies around the world and are invested in others. People look up to you for strength and guidance. They expect you to be a moral god, little *g*, that they can idolize and worship. And you failed."

"I'm not any more perfect than you are, Antoni."

"And it's about time you remember that." His mentor's eyes were sharp.

David packed up his laptop. "We're done here. If you have anything else to say, you can talk to Nathan. At least, I know I can trust him." He took one last look at each of his board members.

"Good day, gentlemen."

———

Bringing his thoughts back to the present, David went to his bar and poured a drink. He watched the amber liquid swirl as he tilted the glass. Then he turned, disgusted, and went to the sink, pouring it out. Alcohol wouldn't solve this problem. He wasn't sure what would.

When he was a teenager, he defended a friend from a large, aggressive kid. His friend had been face down in the school hallway while the bully held his knee on his friend's back. David had used his history book as a weapon, whacking the bully in the head. The larger kid had released his friend and stood, ready to take on David. But David held his ground, the book between them. It was a strange weapon and wouldn't really have been very effective in the long run. But the bully just stared at him before turning to leave. Sometimes, that was all it took with a guy like that.

He became a hero to some that day. Now, he wasn't sure what he was.

His rise up the corporate ladder was rapid, and he quickly became known as a man who ran his business with integrity. When he made a deal, it was fair. Even his enemies did business with him, although begrudgingly. After all, he made money for them, too.

Still, being on top had its challenges. Most of his business partners admired him. Some feared him. And some watched him from afar, waiting for their opportunity to take him down. Had that time come?

He laid down on his couch and tried to practice some of the relaxation techniques offered by his company's mental health department. Their world moved quickly and was stressful. He felt it his duty to offer the service.

Breathing slowly in and out, he tried to clear his mind. But it didn't work. Images flooded his brain. Bright blue eyes. Trusting eyes. Eyes that made him want to wrap the baby in his arms and run away with him. Eyes that scared him half to death.

Now those eyes would be buried in a tiny grave, with a headstone that didn't even list a name. It wasn't fair.

A song popped into his head. He had once liked music. He had once been an accomplished musician. In fact, it was the one thing that soothed his soul when he was trying to study for his final exams.

He had forgotten that.

Striding to his expansive closet, he rummaged through long forgotten items to the very back corner. He shoved aside the boxes and files that should have been shredded long ago. And there it was.

His father had gotten it for him one year for Christmas. He picked up the case, blowing twenty years of dust off it and coughing as the cloud surrounded him. Taking the cased instrument with him to the sofa in the living room, he laid the item on the floor and gingerly opened the black, leather cover. Inside lay the prize.

A Martin D-28.

It wasn't the most expensive guitar to be found, but it was a classic, used by many professional musicians and in studios around the world.

He picked up the instrument and held it gently in his hands, rubbing his fingers over the spruce top and rosewood sides and plucking a few strings. It was out of tune, just like his heart.

He ran his thumbs over his fingertips. His callouses were long gone, having been replaced by the softness of his decades in business. He fiddled with the tuning pegs, careful not to break the strings as they stretched. Finally satisfied with the sound, he began a simple finger exercise before realizing what he was playing.

Closing his eyes, he let his fingers take over, surprised they still knew the song twenty years later.

A verse came to mind from Psalms. The hundred and third chapter. From his days in Sunday School, when the teachers still had them memorizing scripture.

"He remembers that we are dust.
The life of mortals is like grass,
they flourish like a flower of the field;
the wind blows over it and it is gone,
and its place remembers it no more."

He played over and over until his fingers bled. Songs his fingers knew. Songs they made up as they plucked and strummed the strings. Songs that had once soothed his soul. Songs that raised unwanted emotions. Songs that brought tears which streamed down his face against his will. His pain turning to anger, he raised the guitar over his head, determined to smash it against something. Anything. He carried it with him to the terrace, ready to throw it over the side to the street below.

But then he saw her, on her own terrace. Huddled in her glider with a blanket around her, knees hugged to her chest. And he crumpled to the tile floor, gently cradling the guitar like the precious baby she had just lost. He recalled another verse from Isaiah, the twenty-fifth chapter.

"He will bring down your high fortified walls
and lay them low;
he will bring them down to the ground,
to the very dust."

Chapter Twenty

ELIZABETH HEARD a cry from David's terrace and watched him raise a guitar over his head before collapsing to his knees. It was a lonely, mournful sound, reminding her of the cry from the baby in the NICU that was struggling and abandoned. He was crushed.

She thought he deserved it. But did he? She was just as guilty as he was.

She stood from her glider and walked back into her own suite. It was no lonelier today than it had been any other day while Yuri was on his travels. But today, the sumptuous penthouse was dark and brooding, as if it, too, was mourning.

It was a small service at the cemetery for her son. A tiny urn, made from the finest blue marble placed in the same vault alongside Yuri. Her son deserved at least that much. Antoni and Leoni were the only two people who joined her there, along with a minister that spoke a few words about the brevity of life. There was no comfort in the words.

She thought she saw a black limo waiting in the distance while she laid her son to rest. She couldn't be sure it was him, of course. But in her heart, she knew he was there. Why hadn't he claimed his son? She hadn't even given her baby a name, hoping that David might have a change of heart. It was a vain hope, she knew, that sprouted and died along with the child of their lust.

"Baby Boy Yassin" was engraved into the granite face of the vault. Strangers visiting the cemetery would think that he was the son of the man also buried there. Would Yuri mind? Would he be angry, that the son of another man was buried with him? Had he suspected that something was going on between her and David? He had questioned her, stopping just short of throwing accusations. He had been so absorbed in his work that he hadn't seen what was happening right in front of him. She shook off the memory. It didn't matter at this point. Yuri, and her son, both reduced to dust.

It had been two weeks since she gave birth. Seven days since her baby died. Her body was healing, but her soul felt detached. Over the months of her pregnancy, she had begun to look forward to this baby. To the joy he would bring into her life, despite how he was conceived. He had looked remarkably like David, and she secretly found comfort in that. His stark blue eyes, the blue of an iceberg. His little nose and ears. They were all the hallmark of a Kingston.

She wandered around her apartment, stopping to look through her glass doors to the building next door. She had not signed the settlement. Had not touched any of the funds he set aside for her. Doing so would have released him from any responsibility for his part in their affair. At least this way, she still had the tiniest thread of hope that he might still want her. Still had her view of the penthouse across the street. Could still watch his comings and goings.

He had not brought another woman onto his terrace. She could only assume that meant he had not found comfort anywhere else.

When she learned he had visited the baby in the hospital, she had felt a glimmer of something. But he did not come to see her. And his visit to the baby was very brief. A perceptive nurse told her he had come to see the baby, but she said it with no judgment. She simply laid her hand over Elizabeth's and mentioned that David had been there. And Elizabeth had only nodded.

Now she was free to do whatever she wanted. She could go to Israel to visit her family. She could go back to school and finish her

MBA. Her attorney advised her to hold tight. To not make any major decisions for several months. Decisions made during such adverse times were usually errors in judgment. Yuri's life insurance and investments would carry her for many years if she managed her money wisely. In time, she could invest in a new business. She had always wanted to start her own fashion line. Perhaps she and Leoni could go into business together. It was just a thought, for now.

Needing something to do, she wandered into her bedroom, picked up her tablet, and sat down to read a book. A good mystery would occupy her mind for a few hours and give her some respite from her thoughts. But she tossed her e-reader aside when the book was about a secret baby.

She thought she heard an infant cry. But then she realized it was her own wail. Soft, at first, but building as her emotions poured out from her.

It wasn't fair. *God, why did you take him from me? Why are you punishing me like this?* Her eyes fell on the bassinet still sitting in a corner, filled with items for the baby. The tiny socks and onesies that she had already bought. The blue stripes and green dinosaurs she would dress her son in. The tiny blue cap that would keep his head warm. The swaddling blankets. The car seat she purchased online that had more high-tech features than her self-ordering refrigerator. Her maternity clothes hung in her closet, unused. She would ask her maid to donate everything to a crisis pregnancy center.

She laid her hand over her stomach, which was already flat. Curling up into a ball on her white tufted duvet, she stuffed her fist in her mouth and let the tears fall.

———

"David, you have a potential problem."

"Only potential? That's a step up from the way things have been lately."

Like a coward, David had watched from behind the tinted glass of his limo, parked at a distance, as Elizabeth laid their son to rest. There were no cameras around that he could see. He was thankful for that, for Elizabeth's sake. She was virtually attacked by media after Yuri's burial. Carlos, being the ultimate chauffeur, had not said a word, giving David his privacy and a judgment free zone.

He wondered what was being said over a child that was barely a week old. There shouldn't be much of a eulogy, but he hoped they hadn't mentioned him. He would have Carlos go by later to see what name was engraved in the granite.

So what was the potential problem? Was Elizabeth suing him? There was an easy fix for that. He would offer another outrageous settlement.

David brought his thoughts back into focus as Nathan entered his office and strode straight to the leather chair. His look was far too serious. What was up?

"Somebody has been buying up Kingston stock. It looks like a shell corporation, and I haven't been able to determine who is behind it. It is buried behind other corps."

So it wasn't about Elizabeth. "Why would anybody be doing that?"

"Your stock price is low right now. You know the old adage. Buy low, sell high."

David paced to the window. He spent a lot of time, lately, looking out that glass. The view on the street, nearly a thousand feet below where he stood, was the same as yesterday. Everyone in a hurry. Anxious. Horns honking. Eyes glaring. Get-out-of-my-way-I-have-someplace-to-be attitudes. He was one of them.

The footprints of the Twin Towers sat across the street, pools of water surrounded by granite engraved with the names of people who had died in the terrorist attack two decades earlier. What were their lives worth?

"Did you know this building sways up to a foot, each way, on a windy day? And we don't even feel it." Turning, he smiled sadly at his old friend.

"I don't think I understand your point." Nathan frowned.

"On the street below, life is going on like nothing has ever happened. This building sways a full twelve inches from side to side, and we don't even feel it. What are we doing here, Nathan? What is anybody doing here? What is so important that we pay a million dollars every month for a few square feet of high-in-the-sky real estate? What is so important to the people below that they push and shove each other to get wherever it is they are going?"

"Are you okay, David?" Nathan stood and put his hand on David's forehead. "Should I call for medical assistance?"

He shoved Nathan's hand away. "I don't need a doctor."

Turning back to the window, he looked out again, watching a plane approach LaGuardia Airport from several miles away. Twenty years ago, people feared those planes. Feared the people who flew them. Wondered if their building would be the next one to succumb to another attack from a Middle Eastern terrorist group. Now he had just signed a major deal with a nation in the heart of that struggle. And nobody even noticed the planes anymore.

"What are you going to do?" Nathan spoke the words quietly.

"I'm not sure, Nathan." He spun away from the window. "But I promise I am not going to harm myself. In spite of your concern that I need medical assistance." He raised an eyebrow at his attorney and paused before continuing. "I will take your notice about the stock under advisement. I still own forty-eight percent. It will be difficult for anyone to take over without my consent." Walking to his closet, he pulled out his overcoat. "I'll let you know what I decide."

With that, David walked out the door. Nathan was probably stunned. It was still morning. But David didn't care.

————

"Leoni, if my child was so special to God, why did he die? You said he had a purpose."

Elizabeth was being measured for a new design. Her body had changed with the pregnancy, and Leoni wanted it to hang perfectly on her now less than perfect shape. But Leoni said she had a mature, fuller, and more experienced look. Happy, and yet sad. People would relate to that.

"I don't know. But perhaps His purpose was to make you and David think about what you were doing."

"David had already broken off our relationship by the time I realized I was pregnant."

"Yes. But you conceived very early on. Like the first or second weekend together?"

"I guess so."

"So now you are going through all this reflection, thinking about not only your affair with David but your relationship with God."

Elizabeth blinked. Leoni was right.

"And coming to different conclusions?" Her friend smiled softly at her.

"Yes."

"Elizabeth, God still loves you. But sometimes He lets us experience the consequences of our actions."

"When did you get so wise?"

"Experience is a harsh teacher."

"You have three children, though." She looked down at Leoni, who looked back at her.

"I have one in heaven."

"Oh. I didn't know that. I'm so sorry." Elizabeth wiped a stray hair from her face. Life wasn't fair.

"God brought me to my knees, too. But I know He loves me, and He gave me another chance. Have you ever read Ephesians?"

"Some of it. But I haven't exactly been on speaking terms with God." And it had been a very long time since she had picked up her Bible, at all. In fact, she wasn't even sure where it was.

"It's in chapter three. Let me look it up on my phone. Ah. Here it is.

"'For this reason, I kneel before the Father, from whom every family in heaven and on earth derives its name. I pray that out of his glorious riches he may strengthen you with power through his Spirit in your inner being, so that Christ may dwell in your hearts through faith. And I pray that you, being rooted and established in love, may have power, together with all the Lord's holy people, to grasp how wide and long and high and deep is the love of Christ, and to know this love that surpasses knowledge—that you may be filled to the measure of all the fullness of God.'"

"Oh, that's beautiful. A family with God. And a deep love. I never thought about it that way."

"Yes, it is. And it has been very comforting to me over the years."

"Leoni. I need a hug. And I need to hug you." Elizabeth opened her arms, letting Leoni embrace her, and giving the same in return. She felt like a weight had been lifted off her chest. She didn't know what the near future would hold, but she would be okay.

Chapter Twenty-One

The rental agent looked at him with a curious expression as he ran David's no-limit card through the machine.

"How long did you say you would have the car?" The luxury SUV had every possible gadget and feature. If he was going on an extended trip, he might as well be comfortable.

"A couple of weeks. Or longer. Is that a problem?"

"No, sir. We just like to have an end date for scheduling purposes."

"Of course. Let's say a month, then. I can always bring it back sooner."

"Certainly. Will you be travelling far?"

"West." That was the only direction David had in his mind. No destination, and no timeframe either. All he knew was that he needed to get away. To think about everything that happened—and the threats to his company that Nathan mentioned.

The pressure of his decisions, and the resulting impact, was weighing heavily on his mind and heart. Normally, he wasn't impulsive. He counted the cost of everything he did. Calculated and recalculated. It was what made him immensely successful in business. But he hadn't counted the cost before becoming involved with Elizabeth, and now the urge to hide was strong for the first time in his life.

Shouldn't he be staying home, in New York, to fight for what his so-called friends wanted to take away? He took a breath. No. His company would be fine. His stock would recover, eventually. Just a few days of peace, away from the worries of his life, was all he asked.

It was noon when he left the rental agency, and traffic was light. He hadn't even told William he was leaving. His clothes were carelessly tossed into his suitcase, having packed it himself. Nothing fancy. Just jeans, pullover shirts, and comfortable shoes. There was no need for any business attire for the next few days.

Turning off his phone, he would let the calls, text messages, and emails go unanswered. Let them all wonder.

What was it that Horace Greeley said? "Go west, young man." Well, David wasn't exactly young anymore, but he could still go west. After all, his parents lived in Iowa. He could go home. He could have taken the corporate jet, but he wanted anonymity and a time of peace, away from the stresses that he acknowledged were self-inflicted.

He took the interstate highway across New Jersey and into Pennsylvania, the sun overhead as he made his way across the Keystone state. After three hours of driving, he found a truck stop with a small restaurant. He filled himself and the SUV and felt slightly refreshed. His waitress was overwhelmed with the busyness of the day, so after he paid, he approached her on his way out the door and stuffed a hundred-dollar bill in her hand, thanking her for her stellar and friendly service. Five minutes later, he was on the road again.

Catching up with the Pennsylvania Turnpike, he settled in for the next three-plus hours of driving. He remembered travelling across the turnpike as a kid, when his parents decided to take a family vacation to Washington, DC, and the coast. They wanted him to experience the history in the nation's capital and see the ocean. He had seen both plenty of times in his adult years.

The highway twisted and turned though the mountains, the

trees barren of leaves, allowing the sun to shine through the branches, creating a strobing effect. The long, steep inclines, both up and down, made him watchful of the semi-tractor trucks hauling consumer goods across the country. He had a new appreciation for the hard workers who spent their lives on the road. Special lanes were built for their trucks, and he steered clear of them. Runaway ramps were built occasionally at the side of the road for those drivers who were caught unawares of the speed and danger of those long, downhill slopes.

He had been caught unawares. But not of driving. Of life.

The famous Allegheny Tunnel loomed ahead. It was an engineering marvel at the time it was built, carving its way through the mountain and providing a straight path for travelers who would otherwise have had to detour miles around the tall peaks. Darkness engulfed him as he entered through the mouth of the tunnel, and his headlights automatically turned on. The sudden shift from light to dark taunted him with derision as sure as the darkness eating at his soul. The soft music playing through his satellite radio stopped abruptly as the depth of the mountain blocked the signal.

Earth to David. Earth to David. Come in, David.

He felt lost in the sudden silence. It created a cavity in his mind that allowed his thoughts to echo. Taking a breath, he focused on the road in front of him. The silenced stretched, threatening to buckle him.

A mile later, he saw the light at the end of the tunnel and chuckled to himself, feeling foolish. The entire experience felt like an eternity, but in reality had been less than a minute. The radio reconnected to the satellite as he exited the tunnel, soothing instrumental guitar music filling the car once again with its reassuring sounds. Relief filled him as he was reconnected with the world.

After another quick stop just south of Pittsburgh, he found I-70, which he knew would take him all the way across the heartland of America to the Rockies if he wanted to go that far. The high mountain air might be thin, but it might also cleanse the demons plaguing him.

He was losing everything. Elizabeth. His nameless son. And now his business. He had no doubt the vultures pretending to be his friends and supporters would swoop in. Of course, they were also investors and had a significant stake in what happened, but he knew there were at least two board members who would rob him blind if he let them.

Antoni was a different story. His friend and mentor would stand by him, he hoped. Together, they were unstoppable. But if he defected to the other side? Would it be enough to vote David out? He mentally calculated. It would be close.

———

Elizabeth opened the door to her suite, threw her keys on the side table next to the door, and plopped down on the sofa. Her feet hurt from the new shoes Leoni suggested that she model. Whoever designed shoes with six-inch heels needed to wear them for a few hours to experience the torture he was inflicting on women. She didn't care how famous he was. And she knew it was a man. No woman in her right mind would ever design such a wicked device. Then again, women wore them. That didn't say much for her gender.

She slipped the shoes from her feet and tossed them across the room.

"Hello." Pete's squawk was low and subdued. Almost as if he was whispering.

"Hi, Pete." She rubbed her sore toes.

"Baby gone?" His question was sad, like a lonely soul on a never-ending highway.

"Yes, Pete. The baby is gone."

"So sorry. So sorry." Pete's words were quiet, his tone hushed. He shuffled lightly across his perch and back again. Elizabeth padded in her bare feet across the room to the refrigerator for a strawberry. Pete took it from her and bobbed his head. She reached her finger into the cage and scratched the downy feathers under his beak, and he leaned into her touch. It was as if he was trying to comfort her.

How in the world did the bird understand the event that changed her world? Had the maid been talking to him again? She knew parrots were smart, especially macaws. But he couldn't know this for himself, could he?

Yuri told her when he bought the parrot that Pete would be good company. Elizabeth had been skeptical at the time. She had seen online videos of birds that held relatively normal conversations with their owners, if the owners took the time with their bird. She hadn't given the bird that much thought.

She flipped on her television and scrolled through the channels. Between the live on-air channels and the streaming services, she had far too many choices. The news didn't interest her. The action movies had far too much gore, and the romance channels were too sappy.

Even her life in the limelight, wearing Leoni's amazing clothes, didn't satisfy her. She wondered where David was and what he was doing. Stepping out onto her terrace, she looked up at the penthouse suite next door. It was dark, like her soul.

Looking back through her terrace door, she noticed Pete's eyes watching her, his head tilted, his eyes sleepy. With a final glance toward the empty penthouse, she stepped back through her door and zipped the bird's cover closed. At least one of them should get some sleep.

———

The sun set in a brilliant, blinding fireball that slowly slid over the horizon in rays of orange, red, and purple before giving way to the beautiful twilight blue of the coming night. David drove on through the darkness, stars urging him forward unexplainably until exhaustion set in, and he knew he needed to stop. After passing miles of empty fields, he found an exit with a sign for one hotel. The big blue *H* beckoned.

He didn't care about luxury. At this point, he didn't think he deserved it. He pulled into the small parking lot and parked in the only open slot. Why would a town so small have such a busy hotel?

Looking around as he entered, he noticed the lobby was small but clean. A staircase ran from the first floor to the only other floor. The earthy shades of blue and brown décor were pleasing enough, and the lobby had a clean smell. He approached the registration desk, which was empty, and rang a small bell that sat on the counter.

A short, plump woman came out from an office door behind the area. Her gray hair testified of her age, and he wondered why in the world she was working the night shift.

"May I help you?"

"Yes, I need a room, please." He pulled his wallet out of his back pocket.

"Do you have a reservation?"

"Um, no. I wasn't sure I would make it this far tonight."

"One night? Checkout is at eleven a.m."

He looked at the clock, tapping his credit card on the counter. It was already five a.m. He would only get about five hours sleep. And that was if he was able to fall asleep quickly.

"Probably two nights, if you have room. Or more, I'm not sure." He didn't even know what town he was in.

The woman openly stared at him, making him uncomfortable. He did sound a bit unstable.

"I have one open room, but it is the executive suite. More expensive than the others."

David looked down at himself. His clothes were wrinkled from sitting in the car all day. He hadn't shaved before leaving. And he probably didn't smell the best, either. She most likely thought he couldn't afford the price.

"I'll take it."

She raised her eyebrows at him. "I'll need a credit card and ID, please."

He slid the items across the counter, but she didn't indicate any recognition at his name. Just typed in the info without paying any attention to who he was. Well, that suited him just fine. He would rather be incognito.

She handed him two card keys in a sleeve that contained the WiFi password, and pointed to the elevator, which was around the corner from the stairs. "Your room is number two twenty-six. At the far end. Should be good and quiet back there."

"Thank you, ma'am."

He slid the card keys into his shirt pocket and put the ID and credit card back in his wallet. He retrieved his suitcase and took the elevator up the single flight, then walked the long walk down to the other end of the hallway. Entering the room, he glanced around. The king-sized bed with a puffy white duvet took up the center. The air was stale, the temperature a little cool. Probably because this room was rarely used. He adjusted the thermostat on the wall, making sure it was set to heat.

A sitting area with a sofa and TV, desk, and a small kitchenette, along with a serviceable bathroom, made up the front of the suite. A small brown chair and ottoman were placed on the other side of the bed, in front of the window. The view from there included the parking lot and a mom-and-pop restaurant next door. The lighted sign said Debbie's. Open twenty-four hours.

It would do.

He flopped down on the bed, stripping himself of his shirt and pants before crawling under the covers. Winging it wasn't his method of operation, but something about this place drew him in. He decided this small town would be his home for the next few days.

Chapter Twenty-Two

The next morning, after a delicious breakfast at the restaurant of eggs, bacon, toast, and the best hash browns he had ever eaten, David slid into his rented SUV, deciding to drive through the community to see what it had to offer. In the daytime, he could see it was a small town. Traffic moved along the two-lane road at a steady pace. He drove around a town square where an ornate courthouse sat. It was probably over a hundred years old, judging by its architecture and limestone construction. He recalled reading somewhere that Indiana was well-known for its limestone quarries.

He exited the square and took the two-lane road leading west, out of town. A big box discount store, a pizza restaurant, and a small strip mall gave way to an occasional house as he left the small business section. Empty fields filled the spaces between. Old windmills stood tall over a few, but they were not moving, and he suspected they were not functional anymore. Irrigation pipes and crawlers stood silent in some fields, ready for next season.

He knew from his experience growing up in Iowa that the fields had to lay fallow during the offseason to rest. The empty fields looked a lot like he felt.

He'd lost his son. The picture on his phone that he had taken during his one visit to the NICU haunted him. The baby might have called him Daddy. Now he would never hear that word.

He'd lost his son's mother. Their relationship may have started as an affair, but he was starting to realize how unfair to her he had been. Her life had been turned upside down, along with his. And thanks to him, she had lost her baby and her husband.

He was losing his business, the one thing he'd dedicated his entire life to building. Surprisingly, that thought didn't scare him.

But what was left?

He turned randomly, driving aimlessly along the unmarked roads, hoping the GPS would get him back to the hotel. The farther out of town he went, the smaller the roads became and more rural the area.

A buggy came up the road from the other direction, holding a young couple and two small kids. The man was dressed in the typical blue-and-black Amish garb of homemade pants, shirt, and suspenders. His face was shaved in the way of the Amish, as well. Mustache clean, beard trimmed. He smiled and waved. They were all bundled against the cold but didn't act like they noticed it at all.

The woman looked at her husband as if she cherished the ground he walked on. The two boys waved enthusiastically from the back of the conveyance. It was a strange contrast. They had nothing compared to him. Handmade clothes. Horse and buggy. No electricity, or so he had heard. No indoor plumbing in most homes, just an outhouse behind the main structure, and dry sinks in the kitchen. They pumped water from a spigot outside and carried it in using two-gallon buckets. The bishops of the community set the rules for the *Englischer* conveniences they could and could not use. But the smiles on their faces told him they were content.

He took a breath. Would he ever smile again?

He did find peace in the open countryside. No traffic. No city noises. No crowds of people rushing to get to the next place. It made him feel grounded. He opened his sunroof, letting the sunshine in even though it was cold. The fresh air was invigorating.

He had gone several miles through the wandering countryside

when he spied a small church up ahead and decided to stop. It looked like something he might have found in an old prairie novel with its white clapboard siding and stained-glass windows on the side facing the road. He assumed there were more windows on the other side.

Pulling into the gravel lot, he raised his eyes upward to the steeple. It was a square, open-sided box with a spire and a cross on top. Inside was a bell. The old, swinging kind that someone rang each Sunday by pulling on a rope that hung down into the foyer. The clang would ring across the fields, calling the neighborhood to worship. He walked up the concrete stairs, where dips in the steps were worn away by a century or more of attendees as they came and went.

The large double-paneled doors were much like the doors to his apartment. Painted white, they had signs of wear just like the steps. He thought about the generations of kids that ran in and out through those doors, their parents telling them to slow down. It made him smile. Pushing his thumb on the old-fashioned tab, he pulled, surprised when it opened. Did they not lock their doors?

He stepped across the threshold into the small foyer, where he saw the end of the rope that hung from the bell. A coatrack hung on one wall, and a hoodie hung on the rack. Looks like somebody forgot it after last week's service. Or had it been hanging there longer? On inspection, he found dust on the top of the hoodie. He smiled, thinking somebody must be wondering where they put their jacket. Or maybe they had only visited once and were now long gone, the hoodie left behind.

He stepped through the foyer into the sanctuary. The interior made him feel welcome. It smelled of old wood and good times. Perfumes and colognes mingled in the air. He could see the families gathered together in his mind, where there was lots of love, laughter, and friendship. Where people supported each other, not like the cutthroat city. No competition. Just community.

His practiced eye told him the church would seat about a hundred people when full. Two rows of wooden pews led to a small stage at the front of the church. A podium sat front and center of the stage with an embroidered drape over the front that stated, "He is Risen." Lilies surrounded the words in purple, yellow, green, and white. Someone had lovingly made the item.

An old, upright piano sat on one side of the stage. He opened the lid and walked his fingers over the keys. It was out of tune, as he expected. But he bet the pianist played like it was a concert grand piano. He could envision a lively, gray-haired grandmother in a flowery dress and matching hat, banging out the songs with vigor, burning up the keys with hot fingers as they sang "When the Role is Called Up Yonder." That was a song he remembered from his parents' church back in Iowa. The memory made him smile.

Moving off the stage to the front pew, he sat and soaked in the silence. How long had it been since he sat quietly and listened to his surroundings?

He could hear the building breathing.

No, it was not airtight. But it was more than simple air movement. It was generations of memories, breathing in and out. Each pop and crack of a floorboard or moan through a window spoke of a time and era that he thought long gone, but still existed here in the middle of nowhere.

He laid his hand on the wooden seat worn smooth with time and discovered a Bible. A gold embossed name on the front said *Robert Samuels*. The man must have forgotten it after attending the service on Sunday. Did he own the hoodie left hanging on the coatrack?

The black leather cover was cracked from age. The binding was worn, but still holding together. David flipped through the pages carefully and found notes written around the edges. Verses underlined. This book had been well-studied. Loved, even.

Turning to the Gospel of John, he looked for the famous passage. Third chapter, sixteenth verse. It was one most people knew by heart, even if they didn't believe it. But a couple of verses down, he found another verse that made him stop and think.

"Everyone who does evil hates the light,

and will not come into the light
for fear that their deeds will be exposed.
But whoever lives by the truth
comes into the light,
so that it may be seen plainly
that what they have done
has been done
in the sight of God."

His heart caught in his chest. He tried to hide his deeds. By instigating the affair. By bringing Yuri home to Elizabeth, multiple times, to try to cover up the pregnancy. Then by sending him to his death in Jordan. By denying the baby. By telling lie, after lie, after lie.

The truth hit him in the face.

He fell off the bench to his knees, dropping the Bible as he did. Crawling like a child, he made his way to the stage and climbed the three steps on his hands and knees, tears dripping from his eyes. He panted, unable to breathe, until he finally collapsed on the carpeted platform, hands out in front of him, face down, flat on the floor, his sins tormenting him like worms crawling through his brain. His sobs echoed around the sanctuary, his tears added to those of generations before him.

He didn't know how long he laid that way.

Finally, a roar escaped from his lips, and he beat his fist on the floor. It would be bruised tomorrow, but he didn't care. He needed to feel something other than the pain radiating through his heart.

"My son. My son. MY SON! Dear God, why did you have to take my son?

"He was innocent. Made in my image. He may have grown up to be a great businessman. Or a great president. He could have solved the Middle East crisis. Or found a cure for cancer. Why did you take him?"

He continued to cry and beat on the floor, the sobs torn from his throat.

"Take my business. I don't care. Take every dollar I own. I don't care. Take my life. It's worthless anyway. Just take me. All of me. Because I have nothing left."

He wondered what he could do to ease his agony. Turning his face, his eyes sought for something within his limited vision from his position on the stage to take his life with. But he was too weak to even get up, so he turned his head to the other side, where he saw a picture of Jesus hanging on the wall, compassion in the eyes that seemed to see right inside his soul. He didn't deserve forgiveness.

The room grew quiet as David remained there, flat on the floor, spent. The building continued to breathe. A door opened and closed, but David didn't pay attention to the sound. Footsteps fell softly as the intruder walked across the floor and picked up the Bible. David covered his head with his hands, ashamed at being found this way.

A voice began to speak in soothing, low, soft words. The man was reading from the Bible. It sounded like a Psalm.

"'Blessed is the one
    whose transgressions are forgiven,
    whose sins are covered.
Blessed is the one
    whose sin the LORD does not count against them
    and in whose spirit is no deceit.
When I kept silent,
    my bones wasted away
    through my groaning all day long.
For day and night
    your hand was heavy on me;
my strength was sapped
    as in the heat of summer.
Then I acknowledged my sin to you
    and did not cover up my iniquity.
I said, "I will confess
    my transgressions to the LORD."
And you forgave
    the guilt of my sin.'"

His namesake wrote those words centuries earlier, when forced to acknowledge his own sin. His own affair. The man who David worked to emulate had also fallen hard. He sniffed at the irony, and the dust from the carpet tickled his nose. He tried not to sneeze.

The voice spoke again.

"David, get up."

How did the man know who he was? He lifted his head and rolled to sit upright. He rubbed his face with the palm of his hands, then ran his fingers through his hair and blinked to clear his tears, rubbing his thumbs over his eyes.

Sitting on the pew where he had sat moments ago, a man was holding the Bible. His hair was white with age, short and neatly trimmed. His brown eyes held love and wisdom. And David saw no judgment on the man's face.

"I see you found it. I came over to look for it and, well, there you were." The man tapped the Bible in his hands.

"How did you know my name?" David crossed his legs, still unable to stand.

"My wife works the night shift at the hotel. She asked me to pray for you."

"I guess you know everything, then." He bowed his head.

"We do get the news here."

David looked up and nodded. He didn't know what else to say. The man stood and held out his hand to help David to his feet.

"I'm Reverend Samuels. But most people call me Bob."

"That's your Bible, then. You've studied it a lot." David shook Bob's hand.

"I never go anywhere without it. Except, of course, today. God must have wanted you to see it."

David didn't know how to respond. They sat silently on the pew for a few minutes.

"You're the preacher here?"

"I'm not a preacher. I'm a minister." Bob tapped the Bible in his hands again.

"What's the difference?"

"A preacher stands behind a pulpit and tells people they are going to hell if they don't turn from their wicked ways. And while there may be some purpose for that, my calling is to help people find healing from the things that have broken them." He waved his hand to indicate the hundred-year-old building around them. "There's plenty of brokenness here."

"Well, I'm not broken, so I don't need healing. Thanks anyway."

Bob raised his eyebrows.

"Okay. A little broken."

"And you could use a friend? I assure you any conversation between us will remain confidential. Minister-client privilege, you know."

David shrugged. What did he have to lose?

"Would you like to come over to the house for coffee? We live right next door." Bob pointed his thumb over his shoulder.

"That would be nice. Thank you."

He didn't know what would happen with this visit, but he had a feeling he was about to find out.

Chapter Twenty-Three

"What brings you to Indiana, David?" Bob handed him a coffee mug with the face of a Labrador retriever on it. The face resembled that of the dog laying on the kitchen floor, his nose on David's shoe. David took a sip. Strong and black, just the way he liked it.

"I decided to take a road trip. Started driving, spent most of the day on the road, and finally got tired enough to stop. Your little town had the first decent hotel that I came to."

"Hm." Bob took a sip of his own coffee that was laced with cream. "I felt a breeze this morning. The kind of breeze that tells you a change of weather is coming in. God speaks through the breeze, you know."

"The still small voice?" David looked over his coffee cup.

"So you do know your Bible. Or at least, some of it."

"I've tried to live my life by Psalm 127."

"'Unless the Lord builds the house, they labor in vain who build it.'" Bob quoted the verse. "You can't claim ignorance, then, can you? Just . . . misguided?"

David rubbed his hand over the smooth surface of the antique oak dining table. He thought back over his life and wondered how many families had sat around this very table, talking about their lives. Mothers talking to daughters about guarding their hearts. Girls, sisters and friends, giggling over who was the cutest boy at school. Fathers and sons talking about sports, colleges, and those giggly girls. Parents holding hands as they prayed over their children who had gone on to adulthood. Discussions about farm prices. Beef. Corn. Soybeans. A world away from his own daily rat race of board meetings, contract negotiations, New York City steel and concrete.

"Go on."

"There is more to that Psalm." Bob picked up his Bible and turned to the middle of the book.

"'It is in vain that you rise up early
and go late to rest,
eating the bread of anxious toil;
for he gives to his beloved sleep.'"

David looked at the minister. He thought he had relied on God to build his business, but he could see that he had gotten distracted. He allowed the enticements of the world to draw him away. And now he was paying for it.

"Tell me about Elizabeth." Bob's voice was kind.

"There's not much to tell. She was a mistake." David flicked his eyes to the view out the window over the kitchen sink. It was hard to admit his failure.

"What you did together was a mistake. But God's creations are never mistakes. That includes Elizabeth, and you."

David winced. Bob saw through him. His world was falling apart, making him feel like he should never have been born.

"God will restore you, David. But you must give everything back to Him. And I do mean everything. Listen to the rest of the Psalm.

"'Behold, children are a heritage from the Lord,
the fruit of the womb a reward.
Like arrows in the hand of a warrior
are the children of one's youth.
Blessed is the man

who fills his quiver with them!
He shall not be put to shame
when he speaks with his enemies in the gate.'"

David scoffed. "It's a little late for that. I'm getting a bit old to start filling my quiver. And my enemies aren't exactly breaking down the gates to speak to me. They would rather destroy me."

"God is never late, David. But usually, His plans are different from ours."

"So, what are you saying?"

Bob was one of the most compassionate men David had ever met. He oozed kindness. In his appearance, ala Mr. Rogers. In his voice. Soft-spoken today, but he had a feeling the man could raise the roof if need be. And in the way he listened to David. He didn't need to point out David's sin. God had already done that. He simply pointed out that repentance was followed by redemption.

Bob leaned back in his chair. "How long are you staying in town? My wife is not only a stellar hotel clerk, she is also a mean cook. It will give us some time to talk. Do a little fishing. You ever fish?"

"I grew up in Iowa, and I went fishing a couple of times with my grandfather. But I haven't been since I was a kid."

"We've got a great reservoir west of here about thirty miles. And I've got a johnboat. It's not fancy, just a hard seat, a trolling motor that sputters, and a couple of oars in case the motor dies, but it gets the job done."

"Sounds relaxing." He tilted his head in thought. "But how about if I take you two out for a nice dinner this weekend? As a thank you for your hospitality."

Bob scoffed. "There's nothing around here as fancy as you are used to. Besides, nothing beats fried bass straight out of the lake. Or catfish, if we catch one. The bluegill are mighty fine eatin', too. A little bony, but tasty."

David smiled. He remembered his grandfather saying the same thing. "All right, then. I accept your offer."

Mrs. Samuels walked into the room and gave David a hug,

smiling brightly. He shook his head, marveling at how God led him to this little town, and to this family.

He should probably contact Nathan to let him know he was alive, and check in with William, too. But right now, he wanted to enjoy his newfound freedom.

He left the parsonage smiling. He was a lover of music, and while classical was his favorite, today the music was in the nature around him. The warm sun shone on him. Birds sang, their songs blending and filling the air. A dog barked next door; another one down the street gave an answering bark.

The wind blew softly, rustling the brown leaves scattered across the sidewalk between the parsonage and the church, blowing them in a merry dance. Looking up, he spied one floating through the air, having escaped the tree that had borne it. The leaf twirled and flipped, over and over before landing gracefully in a nearby cornfield.

He spread his hands wide and joined the dance as he made his way to the car on the other side of the small church. The hundred-year-old building had seen many confessions and possibly, some like his. He thought of the old adage "if these walls could talk." He finally felt lighter, freer, floating like the leaf above him. New York was hundreds of miles away, and he knew he would have to return to face the music waiting for him there. But first, he would spend a few days here in this small town. Then, he would go to Iowa to see his parents. And eventually, he would have to go home.

———

Elizabeth's phone rang with another unknown number. The media hounds hadn't bothered her since she decided to go public modeling Leoni's designs. She almost didn't answer it, but curiosity got the better of her, so she hit the green button on her screen.

"This is Elizabeth."

"Mrs. Yassin. My name is Charles Haste. I am a business partner with your husband. Or, I was. I am very sorry for your loss."

"Thank you, Mr. Haste. What can I do for you?"

"We met at Yuri's funeral. I was with another business partner. You may not remember us."

"Yes. I do remember you. But I don't understand the reason for the call." This must be one of the two men who said they were Yuri's friends.

"Mrs. Yassin, we were in discussions to buy shares of Kingston Holdings from your husband. We were unable to complete the deal before he died, and we would like to extend the offer to you. I can assure you we will make it very lucrative."

"I didn't know Yuri owned stock in Kingston. But I guess it makes sense. He was a vice president."

"He owned four percent of the total shares. That doesn't sound like much, but I assure you it is significant."

Elizabeth sat on her sofa, thinking about the new turn of events. Why would Yuri have tried to sell it before he died? He was still a member of senior leadership in the company. Was he was trying to sell out so that he and Elizabeth could retire together? Or, was this phone call was a scam?

"Why should I believe you? And why wouldn't you have gone through his attorney? Or his financial advisor?"

"You own the stock now. We thought it best to approach you first. As a courtesy."

Her head was spinning. She didn't know much about the stock market, but she knew people bought and sold every day. But didn't they go through brokers? This was way out of her comfort zone.

Something was going on, but why was her stock so important? If buyers wanted it, she needed to investigate this matter further before taking action, either way.

"Mr. Haste. I appreciate your offer. But I need to think about this before I do anything. Give me a few days. A week or two. I want to find out what I own and get advice from people I trust before making any decisions. I owe that much to my husband."

"I certainly think that is wise, Mrs. Yassin. Yuri would be proud of you for proceeding with caution. And I do advise caution here.

There are sharks in the market that would steal your stock for pennies on the dollar. At any rate, you have my number now. Please give me a call if you have any questions at all. I assure you my partners and I will pay a premium rate for the stock, should you choose to sell."

Elizabeth took a deep breath as Mr. Haste ended the call and let it out slowly. She would sit on this request for a while. Her attorney advised her not to make any major decision for at least a year. Her heart told her this was one of those decisions, worth millions of dollars. There was no hurry to do anything.

———

David said goodbye to Reverend and Mrs. Samuels, wishing he could stay longer. His days with the minister and his wife were filled with a lot of conversation, fishing, and relaxing on their front porch. They listened to the mockingbirds mimic the sounds of various birds during the day, and the whippoorwills call back and forth to each other while the sun set behind the corn field each night. He kept his phone turned off for most of the visit, but he did inform William and Nathan where he could be found. His assistant was very discreetly managing his calendar, while Nathan fielded any questions from business partners.

The drive to his parents' home in Iowa was another eight hours. But this trip was different. He kept his radio tuned to upbeat music. Sometimes classical, sometimes country or top-forty Christian, but always cheerful. The mood matched the lightness in his heart. He was ready to spend a few days with his parents, and then he would go home and accept whatever waited for him there.

———

Elizabeth stared at the large, thick envelope in her hand. Nine-by-twelve, it held the official seal of Kingston Holdings. It was the second one with the Kingston name on it that she had received this year. The last one was the invitation that started it all.

The return address on this envelope said it was from the Board of Directors, and it had been delivered by special courier.

Did she dare open it?

She flipped it over and looked at the sealed flap, wondering what she would find inside. Was she being sued? Would the board try to hold her accountable for the slide the company was experiencing? She hadn't been the one to tell the world about the baby, but the media had eaten it up, creating suppositions and stories that had absolutely no relevance to the truth. Even though she modeled Leoni's gowns at special events, smiling for the cameras, she spent many of her days hidden inside her penthouse suite, feeling like a prisoner. It was a strange paradox.

The maid continued to stop by each morning, leaving at exactly seven fifty-five as scheduled. Leaving Elizabeth alone. She should get up early tomorrow. Talk to her maid and spend some time with her. Actually get to know her, instead of taking for granted that she would always be there. Yes. That was exactly what she would do.

One decision made, she stared at the unopened envelope again. Was it information about the trust? Since she hadn't contacted her attorney, perhaps the board decided to reach out to her. That would be a positive. But she recalled meeting some of them at the gala, and again at Yuri's funeral. Some of them were more like shysters than anything else.

She thought of the phone call from the other man she met at Yuri's funeral. Two men who said they were friends of her husband, but she had never met them. As little as she knew about his business life, she realized there were large gaps in what she knew about his personal life, too. Especially his more recent comings and goings. The man said he wanted to buy Yuri's stock. Did this envelope have something to do with that?

She walked into her office, which she rarely used since she had assistants to manage her mail, finances, and other business. But she rarely saw them, as well. This envelope, however, was addressed specifically to her. Hand delivered by special courier. She opened the drawer of her small desk and pulled out a letter opener.

The mother of pearl handle on the antique gleamed in her hand. It was handed down to her from her grandmother, who was buried in a grave somewhere back in Israel. The silver blade reflected her brown eyes. She slipped the blade under the sealed flap of the envelope and began to slide.

The envelope opened cleanly.

Taking a deep breath, she laid down the opener and peaked inside the envelope, leery of what she would find inside. Finally, she closed her eyes and pulled out the thick packet of pages.

On top was a cover letter. The board was seeking her proxy. But for what?

Elizabeth knew Yuri held a little stock in the company. Charles Haste said it was four percent, but she didn't know how much that really was. But with first Mr. Haste's phone call, and now this letter, his shares were apparently important. She continued to read through the legalese, scanning the pages until she got to the final, most important, page.

The board wanted to oust David as CEO.

Chapter Twenty-Four

"David!" His mother ran from the house as soon as he pulled into the driveway. The curtain had fallen from the window, and the door was flung wide, despite the weather. Iowa was cold in December, but his parents flew at him like it was balmy.

He relished the feeling of being in his mother's arms, even as a middle-aged man. Her soft hug and warm scent wrapped around him, bringing memories of the many times she comforted him. After a bicycle accident. Or his first girlfriend. After Abigail left him. And again with Allison. Her perfume was the same kind she always bought from the makeup aisle of the local pharmacy. Her consistency never failed, and he loved her all the more for it. Coming home had been the right thing to do.

He shook his father's hand, noticing the lines around his eyes and the silver in his hair. But his grip was as strong as ever. His father always taught him that his handshake was as good as his word and should be just as strong and true. David grinned as their eyes locked. He was glad to be here.

Dinner was also as filling as he remembered it being. His mother had not lost her touch. Between Mrs. Samuels's meals and his mother's, he would have to schedule time with his personal trainer when he went back to New York. He chuckled, thinking about the horrified faces he would see on his trainer and his tailor, who would likely have to adjust his suits. He had always been fastidious about his health. But his time away was just what the doctor ordered. He was more relaxed than he had been in years.

"Where have you been the past couple of weeks? I tried to call you a few times, and you didn't answer." His father asked the question between bites of chocolate pudding layered between whipped cream and a graham cracker crust. Around here, it was called Mud.

"It's a long story, but I've been in Indiana. Reflecting on my life. I guess you've seen the news. Heard everything."

His dad stood and walked to a small desk in the corner. He returned with a large white envelope.

"We got this in the mail last week. Your voice mailbox was full, so I called your office, but they said you were out of town."

David examined the thick, nine-by-twelve envelope. The return address said, "Board of Directors," followed by Kingston Holdings' address. Flipping it over, he lifted the flap that his father had already opened, knowing in his heart what must be inside. His suspicions were confirmed when he pulled the papers from the envelope.

"You have stock in my company?"

"We have always followed you, David. Always wanted to support you. Our stock amount is small and probably won't have any bearing on what is going on, but if we got this notice, the other stockholders would have received it, too. Are you selling your company?"

The names on the last page listed all the board members, with Antoni's name on top. He was behind the coup?

"It looks like Antoni wants the company back."

"I thought he was your friend."

"Yeah. Well, you know what they say about friends and enemies." They had been friends for nearly twenty years. Stood side by side as they grew the business, sharing valuable advice. From Antoni to David, and David to Antoni.

His father laid his hand on David's arm. "Is this about the woman?"

A sigh escaped him. "Elizabeth is his granddaughter. But I didn't know that until just recently. I'm not sure why it was so secret. He keeps a picture of the two of them when she was much younger on his desk, but he never told me who it was. Thinking back, I see the resemblance now."

"And the baby was his grandson?"

"Great-grandson." He rubbed his chin, sliding his hand down to his neck and around to the back. The pinch in his shoulders was back.

"He was our grandson, too. Tell us what happened." His father's eyes held undeserved compassion.

He pulled his phone out and flipped to the picture he had taken in the NICU, handing it to his father, who shared it with his mother. As far as he knew, it was the only picture of his son. Not holding back, he gave them every sordid detail. His parents listened quietly as he spun the story, stopping to close his eyes and breathe as he relived the events in his mind. An hour later, his parents pulled him to his feet and hugged him from both sides. They would love him forever, no matter what. If only he had learned that lesson sooner.

But now he was free. He had to remember that, and not let the darkness come over him again. Even a single candle could dispel the darkness. He would not let this new light go out.

———

The private jet winged its way across the sky as David took what would likely be his last flight on this luxury aircraft.

He recalled his time spent in Indiana, visiting with the Samuels family, and learning a lot about life, love, forgiveness, and salvation from them. The minister had provided valuable insight that David would never forget, and his wife was equally as gracious.

There was one conversation they had while fishing on a small lake in a heavily wooded forest. State forest, if he recalled Bob's description. The seats of the johnboat were hard, even with the blue vinyl boat cushions, which had seen many decades of use. The rods and reels were almost as old, and the bait was slimy nightcrawlers and creepy crawly crickets. He fished as a kid, but they used lures. This was different.

Bob told him a Bible story he had never heard, about when the tax collector came around and the disciples had no money to give him. Jesus told Peter to cast his line into the Sea of Galilee, where they were camped, and bring in the first fish. It had a coin in its mouth. Enough to pay the taxes.

Bob didn't even tell him what the story meant. But David knew. He built his life around money, and the influence that money brings. Could he give it all up? Trust God for the outcome? He smiled, recalling the day. The warm sunshine. Soft breeze. And company of a quiet man who lived his Bible as much as he preached it.

His visit home had not been nearly long enough. He had stayed a few days with his parents, soaking in their unconditional love. They nurtured his spirit as they laughed with him over good memories and cried with him over love lost. He made a mental vow to make regular visits going forward. But he had to get back to his life. To his company. To whatever awaited him in New York.

He and his parents had a long discussion during his visit where he offered to buy his father's firm in Iowa. He could start over. Give his parents a chance to retire. In their sixties, they were ready to travel and see the world. He would make sure they had anything they wanted. Then he would rebuild. It was hard to leave, but the clock was ticking.

The board was voting tomorrow, and he knew without a doubt that he would no longer be CEO of Kingston Holdings, Inc. Instead of letting God build the house, as his mission statement stated, he had built a house of cards. And it was falling down.

Oh, he would still own nearly half the company, but without being at the helm it would no longer be his to control. The board would choose another person, probably from outside the company, to run it according to their direction. They would offer him a buyout, and he would sell. No sense hanging onto the memories.

As for Elizabeth, he wished her all the best. He accepted full responsibility for everything. The trusts had already been established, so they were not at risk. She was a beautiful, resourceful woman and would land on her feet. In fact, it looked like she already had. The Leoni gowns she wore to the theater and charity events were stunning and provided a lot of exposure for the designer.

He and Nathan were good friends as well as business partners. He would keep his attorney on retainer for personal business. The man had a level of integrity that far surpassed his own sorry excuse for the moral value. He shook his head, not allowing that thought to grab him. He was a new man.

The flight attendant was efficient. Benjamin was working his way through flight school, and David chuckled as he remembered boarding and finding the young man instead of the certified masseuse. He wondered what happened to her, but she worked for the service that also provided the pilots. It was not his problem to solve.

"Sir? We are on approach."

"Thank you, Benjamin. This will likely be my last flight on this plane."

"For what it's worth, it has been a pleasure." Benjamin shuffled his feet slightly. "You are a good man, Mr. Kingston. I hope everything goes well for you."

So, the young man also followed the news.

"Thank you, Benjamin. A bit of advice? Always strive for integrity. Money and power are dangerous things to have."

"Yes, sir."

David prepared for landing, physically and mentally. As the jet touched down on the private airstrip, he cleared his heart and mind of any malice. It would do him no good to harbor bad feelings for the board, or guilt for everything he had done. After all, he was forgiven by the One who had the power to forgive. The plane taxied to the small terminal where an SUV was waiting.

He said goodbye to the flight crew. They would receive a large bonus. As he stepped into the SUV and took the last ride to his penthouse, he began counting the cost of the last few months in his mind. His condo would bring a tidy sum. New York real estate had sky-rocketed in the last few years, and he estimated it would sell for ten times what he paid for it twelve years ago.

The ride up the private elevator caused him to think. Why was everything he did of a solo nature? Private jet, private car, private elevator. He realized he had isolated himself by doing so, and that may have contributed to his downfall. He made a mental note to make himself more publicly available when he moved to Iowa. Not as in the public eye, where social media followed his every move, but friendly. Waving to people on the street. Serving in various ministries at his parents' church. In person, not just with a monetary donation. Eating at the local diner and tipping the waitress. Shopping for his own groceries at the chain store. He wanted to be normal. Not wealthy.

Finally entering his suite, he collapsed onto his soft leather couch and waited for the phone call that would end his career with Kingston Holdings, Inc.

Chapter Twenty-Five

"You didn't return the proxy." Antoni paced across Elizabeth's penthouse.

"No, I didn't."

"Why?"

"I'm going to the meeting tomorrow." She watched him wear a path across her tile floor.

"That's not necessary."

"Yes, it is. I want to know what this is all about. Why is it necessary for this hostile takeover? After all, the affair wasn't entirely his fault. It was mine, too."

"Yuri wasn't your fault."

"No, Yuri was Yuri's fault."

"We need your vote, Liza." Her grandfather picked up the envelope he had slung on the table and held it under her nose.

"David built the company." She shoved his hand and the envelope away.

"No. I built it. He stole it from me."

"You were his mentor for many years. He bought the company from you fair and square. How is that stealing it?"

"He only paid half what it was worth."

"He bought a much smaller company and built it into an empire."

"With investors, including me and my money."

"And you've been harboring a grudge all this time? Why did you continue to work with him, then?"

"As a board member, I still had input into the direction that the company took. I could influence his decisions. Until the Jordan deal. I counseled against it."

"Why do you need my vote, anyway? My shares only equal four percent. Don't you already have enough to take over?"

He faced his granddaughter and placed a finger under her chin, bringing their eyes into focus. "Liza. The sheikh over there wanted you as part of the deal. I happen to know David called you to discuss it, but you didn't answer."

Elizabeth jerked her head away. "He was going to sell me?"

"No, that would have been illegal. But convincing you to become one of Abdullah's wives would have been a great way to get rid of you."

"I don't believe you." She paced away from him to the door.

"Sign the proxy, Liza." Antoni stabbed the white envelope hard with his finger.

"No."

"You would defy your grandfather?" A vein bulged in his neck.

"I'm not defying anyone. I just want to make sure I'm doing the right thing." She stopped, putting her fingers to her temples to calm herself. "I want the opportunity to review the evidence and determine for myself what should be done. I want the details, no matter how ugly. Surely, as a man of discernment, you can understand that."

"You're still in love with him, aren't you?" Antoni's voice shook. "After everything he did to you. You still think you love him. How could you?" Antoni stood in front of her, his eyes narrowed and his arms crossed.

She stared back at him. She got her stubborn nature from him, after all. He seemed to forget that.

"You think he loves you? Do you think he ever loved you? He just wanted a fling. And you gave it to him. Then he left you, high and dry, to deal with the consequences. He didn't even acknowledge the baby.

"What was it your grandmother, God rest her soul, used to say? 'Why buy the cow when you can get the milk for free?'"

Elizabeth was infuriated. She backed away, her eyes wide and the gold flecks in her dark brown irises flaring. "Are you calling me a cow?"

He walked away, his hands bunched into fists, then turned and walked back. "Sign the papers, Liza. All I need is your signature. In fact, I will give you half of my shares of the company if you sign right now."

"I know what this is. This is a power grab. Stinking, filthy greed. Well, I don't need your money any more than I needed his." She crossed her arms and tilted her head, examining his expression. He was serious. Desperate, even. Why was it so important that he would give up half his shares? There must be billions riding on this.

"What do you mean, you don't need the money? Of course you do."

"He offered me a settlement. The kind that would have made even your eyes bug out."

"And you turned it down?"

"Flat." She thinned her lips to match her statement.

"Well, girl, that is proof right there that you don't know what you are doing. Sign the proxy." He softened his voice, but his eyes were still as hard as steel.

"Get out."

Brown eyes locked with brown eyes.

"Liza, this is your opportunity to right a grievous wrong. Multiple wrongs. Against you, Yuri, the baby."

"You know, somebody else offered to buy the stock." She smiled, watching the confused look on her grandfather's face. She didn't know why that pleased her, but it did.

"When did this happen?"

"A few weeks ago. I told him I needed to think about it. I'm glad I did." She raised one eyebrow, her implication clear.

"Who made the offer?"

"A man named Charles Haste."

"I know that name. He does special work for David. All the more reason for you to sign the proxy now."

"No. All the more reason for me to not sign." Elizabeth stood her ground. But Antoni's comment made her wonder. Why would David send someone in his place to buy her shares? Something was going on, and she refused to sell or sign until she had a firm understanding of the impact of her decision.

"I will be there tomorrow, bright and early. And then, you will get your blessed vote." She opened the door. The classic signal of "it's time for you to leave."

Antoni left the envelope on her table and walked out.

Questions rambled through her mind as she closed the door behind her grandfather. She didn't believe for a moment that David would have done what her grandfather suggested he wanted to do. Sell her out to a sheikh for a piece of land? No. He may have tried to deny his baby, but he would never stoop as low as that. And if she had received such a ludicrous offer as to join the sheikh's harem, she would have snorted at it. She was from Israel, for Pete's sake. Her grandfather must be getting doddy in his old age.

Which brought her back to why they wanted to force David out. Why the power grab? She didn't think it was truly about his morality clause, either. After all, she was just as responsible for their affair as he was. And the other board members? Well, she knew things about them, too. None of them were perfect.

Elizabeth crossed the room to Pete's cage. Other than being fed by the maid daily, the poor bird had been neglected lately. She watched him shuffle across his perch, his colorful feathers ruffling as he did. The vibrant reds on his head and upper half blended with yellow and green before turning to blue on the end of his wings, rump, and tail. The giant macaw jumped onto the bars of the cage and tilted his head back and forth as he looked back at her.

"Hello, Pete."

"Hello, Pete!"

"What am I going to do?"

"What to do. What to do."

She sighed, long and slow, and Pete mimicked the sound.

"Oh, Pete. Who do I trust?"

"Trust God."

"What?" Did he just answer her question? No, that couldn't be. She wasn't really talking *to* the bird. It was just a rhetorical question. Just thinking out loud.

"Trust God."

Elizabeth stared at the bird. Where did he get that phrase? She looked around the empty apartment. There was no one here except herself and the bird. Was the maid talking to him again? If so, had she taught him that?

"Trust God!" His shrill whistle shrieked. Shrill and insistent.

She sat down at her dining table and put her head in her hands. The vote was early the next morning, before Wall Street's opening bell, which she assumed was a calculated action. Manage the timing so that the stock price would change after the vote, not before. It would likely go down again, stock would be traded furiously, and the price would rise to the sky. The board members would all be immensely rich.

Using her beauty as an asset would be her best approach. She had to look stunning, yet in charge. She didn't want dark circles under her eyes and couldn't afford to toss and turn all night in worry. She should take the bird's advice.

She walked back into her bedroom and opened the drawer of her nightstand. There in the back was the book she had ignored for too long. It was a present from her mother on her eighteenth birthday. Her mom said that if she ever found herself in trouble, she would find her answers in this book. Elizabeth pushed aside a small notebook, her tablet, phone charger, and several pens and pencils to reach her mother's gift.

The leather cover was soft in her hands, its lavender and green containing a small border of white jasmine flowers. Her favorite. Finding a bookmark, she opened the pages to the purple ribbon and found a proverb that was underlined in red.

"Trust in the Lord with all your heart

and lean not on your own understanding;

in all your ways submit to him,

and he will make your paths straight."

A note was written in the same red ink, followed by a small heart. Elizabeth smiled at the handwriting.

"I love you. Mom."

She traced the words and the heart, smiling to herself. She still didn't know what to do. There were no flashing lights signaling Yes or No. Walk or Don't Walk. No magic fairy waving a wand and writing the answer into the air for her to read. No email, text message, or hashtag from God. But a peace came over her. She would give the problem to Him and sleep easier tonight.

Chapter Twenty-Six

Elizabeth stopped in the doorway the next morning, the envelope in her hand. The executive boardroom simmered with testosterone and cologne. Even at this early hour, the men in tailored suits and red ties exuded importance and power. Coffee cups filled the spaces in front of each man, the rich, black aroma overpowering to her nose. She wished she had her own blend here today.

She could still sign the proxy and walk away. Or, she could stay for the meeting. Choosing to stay, she took a breath, drew herself up as tall as her short five-foot three-inch frame could manage in her stilettos, and entered the room. Five pairs of eyes followed her as she found a seat in front of the window. The boardroom had a stunning view of the harbor, but she wanted to be able to see everyone in the room. The walls were paneled and papered in shades of gray. Black-and-white photos of various offices from around the world hung on the walls, with an occasional red accent as a focus feature in the picture. She smiled at the décor. They were David's favorite colors.

The orange glow of the early morning sun bounced off the overcast sky, turning each face of the waiting men into an apparition. The glow at her back, she studied David's adversaries. The men who were supposed to be his friends and business partners were now poised as his enemies. The giant killers were all eager to take down the giant. They grinned at her like lions salivating over a lioness in heat. She straightened her designer jacket, glad she had chosen a conservative navy blue suit. Nothing to see here. Perverts.

"Good morning, gentlemen. And lady." Antoni nodded to her from her left. The men responded with nods.

"Nathan, where is your client?" The attorney sat on the other end of the table, at her right.

"I have been given power of attorney to vote on his behalf." He laid the notarized document on the table.

"All right then." Her grandfather looked around the room. "We have one item to discuss today. That is the removal of David Kingston as CEO of Kingston Holdings, Incorporated. Is everyone ready to vote?"

"Excuse me." Elizabeth raised her hand. "I have a lot of questions. But I will start with this one. How can you remove the man who owns the company? His name is on it."

The lions turned her direction. Grayson practically snarled, curling his lips with a quick flick of his tongue. James leaned forward to stare at her, hands resting on the table. He looked ready to pounce. But she would not back down. It was a valid question.

The senator, however, leaned back in his chair and studied her, one finger tapping his lips. What was his game? She couldn't read his expression. Could she sway him? And if so, would it be enough?

"We talked about this yesterday, Liza. David owns a plurality of the stock, which means he owns more than any other board member. But he doesn't own a full majority. He only owns forty-eight percent." Antoni spoke like a patient grandfather.

She frowned, thinking through the explanation. "Who owns the rest?"

"I own twenty-four percent. Grayson and James each own eight percent. The senator over there owns seven percent. And you own four percent. That is in round numbers, of course. There are a lot of much smaller stockholders, but the total there is less than one percent. All but one have returned their proxies. But he is not here today, so an absent vote will be placed on his behalf, which tilts the numbers slightly in our favor." Antoni pointed to a stack of documents on the credenza behind him.

"Correction." Nathan spoke up, holding another document. "I have the remaining proxy. From David's father."

Antoni shrugged. "It's not enough to make a difference."

Elizabeth looked back and forth between them. "What does it take to vote him out?"

"It takes more than his forty-eight percent, assuming he votes for himself." Antoni glanced at Nathan, who nodded. "All our votes add up to that same amount. Your four percent will break the tie and clearly take us over fifty percent. It would be no contest."

A light bulb went on. Now Elizabeth understood the offer from Mr. Haste. Her four percent would give David a clear majority. Or was he also testing her loyalty? He would expect her to side with her grandfather. But the other board members didn't know about the offer.

"Unless David is ready to sell out, without the need for a vote. At a rock-bottom price, of course." The senator offered that advice. He was leaning back in his chair, one ankle over the other knee, flipping an ink pen in his hand. His face was made for poker, but she could see the agenda behind his eyes. Like a stealth bomber, prepared to drop the death knell on anything that would suit his purposes. He was a man who wanted to win.

"It would save us all a lot of trouble." Grayson speared Nathan with a look. There was nothing stealthy about his facial expression. It was pure greed. Nathan remained silent.

Elizabeth looked around the room and considered the stakes. A painting of David hung on the wall behind Antoni, just over his head. Her grandfather had also been his friend and mentor, at one time.

She turned in her seat to look out over the harbor. The view from the seventy-third floor was spectacular. Large cargo ships and fancy yachts vied for space as they navigated the channel. Who owned those ships, and how would they vote if they were in her position?

The light shifted as the sun rose over the harbor, the band of orange cutting a slice through the clouds. Torn, she turned back to the men.

"You have been his friends for nearly two decades. Why do you want to do this now?"

James smiled, but it was a slimy gesture, making her feel soiled. "You were a child when we started this venture. You have no idea how we have fought and scrapped over the years."

She tilted her head. "I'd say that makes me less biased. More able to see the facts."

"I don't think it is facts you are interested in, Elizabeth. You did, after all, have his baby." Grayson looked hungry, ready to take down his prey.

"A baby that he refused to acknowledge." James's grin was cunning, but she knew the tactic. Band together to isolate your target. Why didn't her grandfather speak up in her defense? She shifted her gaze to the third man.

"Senator?" She looked at the statesman, who was examining a fingernail. "Don't you have anything else to say? Any other poisoned darts to shoot at me? I hear venom is on special right now." The snarky remark slipped out unheeded. If they could dish it out, she could give it back.

"Oh, I find this to be an interesting little game." He looked up, his copper-colored eyes glowing like a rattlesnake ready to strike. "But the fact remains that we can still make things very difficult for David, regardless of your vote. You are in over your head. It will be better to just give your proxy to Antoni and get it over with."

"In over my head? You think that I don't have a smidgeon of a brain, do you? I reviewed the stock. It did go down for a while, but it is steadily climbing back up." She looked around the room. "You want to shoot a man while he is down, don't you? Take over while the stock price is still lower so you can add to your billions. But what happens to that stock when the word gets out that David has been kicked out as CEO? It will plummet again. That's what."

"You are just a little girl playing dress-up," Grayson snarled.

"But a very lovely little girl. I'll play dress-up with you," James drooled.

"Pigs. That's what you both are." She spit the words out, making her point.

"David sent Charles Haste to you to buy the stock clandestinely. He tried to undercut us." Antoni's face turned red.

"Isn't that what you are trying to do with this vote? Force him out?" She glared back at her grandfather.

"Liza." Antoni issued the warning.

Elizabeth twisted her face to the attorney. "Nathan? What does David want?"

"This isn't about what David wants, Liza."

Elizabeth ignored her grandfather's comment and kept her eyes on Nathan. Did he know about the offer from Mr. Haste? As David's attorney, he could have been behind it.

Nathan straightened, arms resting on the table. His gaze was steady, his eyes compassionate.

"The choice has to be yours, Elizabeth. I'm not going to try to twist your arm, either way. David wants you to have a clear conscience."

Elizabeth considered Nathan's statement. He had not flinched at all. Was the choice really hers to make? What would happen to David if he lost his company? And did she really want to see him lose everything? Everyone else in the room seemed to be ready to boot David to the street, waiting for her to provide the final kick to the gut.

This must be the revenge that Antoni had spoken of. David would still walk away rich, but he would no longer be the man envied by his competitors around the world. His case studies would be removed from business school curriculums. His charities would die, and the recipients of those charities would suffer. He would be cast out of New York as a failure. All because of her. She could not deny her part in his downfall.

A tear slid down her cheek. She knew the lions in the room would see it as a sign of weakness, that she was "in over her head," as the senator stated. But she was helpless to stop it. No matter what she did, somebody would be hurt. But the lions didn't care. They were already moving in for the kill.

She glanced down at the white envelope, still in front of her. If she signed it, it wasn't the same as casting a vote, or was it? She was just giving her vote to somebody else. She could sign the document and walk away before she even heard the final tally. Would that absolve her of any responsibility for the fallout? She placed a white, glittery fingernail on the envelope and watched the paper twirl on the surface of the glass and steel table as she moved her finger in a circle. The room was silent, but the men were getting restless.

"Are you ready, Elizabeth?" Her grandfather pulled her attention back to him. "We need to wrap this up. It won't be nearly as painful as you think it will be, and it will right a great wrong. David gets what he deserves. And you get justice." His eyes were soft, but with a hint of steel.

She closed her eyes and remembered the verse she read last night. She still had no clear-cut answer. It all came down to her conscience. Her trust that God was still in control of the situation. Was this how He would bring David to his knees?

A sunbeam broke through the clouds. She swallowed and nodded, ready to cast her vote. She just hoped she wasn't making a huge mistake.

Chapter Twenty-Seven

David picked up his phone to look at the notice coming through from his security system. The elevator was on its way up. He assumed that Nathan had chosen to deliver the news in person so he opened his white ten-paneled door, ready to absorb whatever blow would be delivered by his attorney.

The elevator opened, and Nathan stepped out. But he wasn't alone. Elizabeth walked out in front of him. They both had serious looks on their faces, and Nathan carried his ever-present briefcase.

David scrunched his forehead, confused.

"You look like you have a lot to discuss. Come on in."

Nathan nodded and waved his hand to Elizabeth to enter first. She scooted sideways through the door, careful not to touch David. Taking a breath of her sweet perfume, he closed his door behind them.

He led them to the dining table, where they could sit comfortably and spread out whatever documents he needed to sign to close out his reign. The era was over, and he almost breathed a sigh of relief. But he would find out the details before he fully relaxed.

Nathan spoke first. "I guess you are curious about the outcome of today's vote. It did not go as expected."

David frowned. "What do you mean?"

"The vote was forty-eight to forty-eight. Elizabeth had the deciding four votes."

"And?" David looked back and forth between them.

"I voted for you, David. I voted to keep you."

"Why?" He turned to face her. "I thought surely you would see this as your opportunity to exact retribution." He crossed his arms in question.

"This is going to sound strange, but I felt uncomfortable about what they wanted to do to you. Something wasn't quite right. So"—she took a deep breath—"I asked my bird what to do."

"Excuse me? Your bird?"

"Well, he does speak, you know. And it wasn't like I was seeking some kind of psychic guidance or anything like that. I was just talking through the situation with myself, and he started answering. At first it was just his normal repetition of everything I said. But then he said, 'Trust God.'"

"Trust God?"

"Yes. I've never heard him say that before now. And he said it multiple times. I've never really believed in signs, but this felt different. Like he really did have a message from God."

David was stunned, his brain whirling with what he had just learned. He stood and paced around the table, his hands behind his back.

"I don't get it." He raised his hands in surrender.

"I didn't either," Nathan spoke up.

"Can I ask you something? Did you really try to sell me to that sheikh in Jordan?" Elizabeth peeked from under her eyelashes.

He stopped his pacing. "What? No. Where did you hear that?"

"I didn't think so."

He looked gently at her. "Who told you that, Elizabeth?"

She stared back at him, pain in her eyes. "My grandfather."

"Antoni."

"Yes."

He was tired of lies. There were too many. "The sheikh saw your pictures on social media. He was pretty taken with you, saying you had the look of an Arab princess. I didn't tell him you were Israeli. That would not have gone over well."

"So what happened?"

"He wanted to meet you. As part of the deal. They, um, women are for the most part personal property over there. He has a harem of them."

"And he wanted to make me part of his harem?"

David nodded.

"Did you really try to call me about it?"

He looked up at the ceiling, then back at Elizabeth's face. She deserved the full truth.

"I did dial your number. Not while in the meeting with him, but back at the hotel. You declined the call, as I suspected you would. I didn't think you would want to talk to me, anyway. But that allowed me to tell the sheikh truthfully, or at least partly so, that I called you and you declined."

"I see. And you got the deal, anyway?"

"We had to sweeten the financial side of the agreement, but yes. We got the deal." He leaned over the table to look directly at her. "I would never have asked you to meet him. I would never treat you that way."

He paused, taking in her brown eyes and allowing his gaze to make his point until she swallowed and nodded. Satisfied with her response, he turned back to Nathan. "What happens now?"

Nathan picked up two documents. "James and Grayson both resigned, effective immediately. The showdown was epic. She really put them in their places. Called them both pigs. They offered their shares to you, at an inflated price, of course, and I accepted on your behalf. I just need your signature here and here." He pointed at the pages.

David chuckled, amused at Nathan's descriptive account. "What else?" He signed the documents as they spoke.

"The senator switched sides faster than a jackrabbit on steroids. You know politicians. They always like to be on the winning team."

"No surprise there." David tapped his finger on the table. "And Antoni?"

"He left immediately after the vote. He was angry, of course. I don't know where he went."

David turned to Elizabeth. "And you? Are you okay?"

"It was difficult, but I'm okay. I know I made the right decision. But I just have one more question."

"What's that?"

"Who is Charles Haste? Did you send him to buy Yuri's stock?"

He nodded, along with Nathan. "I knew as far back as the gala that something was going on. Then Nathan discovered someone buying stock, and we had a feeling they were going to attempt a takeover. Owning Yuri's stock would have secured the majority. It was also a nice test to see how things might go. I hired Haste to investigate and test the waters."

"Why didn't you just come directly to me?" Was that hurt in her eyes?

"Would your answer have been any different?"

"No. Probably not. I was just trying to make sure I did the right thing by understanding the risks first." She looked down at the table as she answered.

"You will make a good board member, Elizabeth." He moved around the table to stand right in front of her, forcing her to look up.

"Do you think so?"

"Absolutely." He sat down again in the chair next to her and focused on her incredible brown eyes.

"You know, I was fully prepared to sell everything and move back to Iowa. My parents are wanting to retire, and I was going to buy them out. I may still do that."

"I would like to meet them someday."

David considered her statement. "I think they would like that, too."

They talked about the rest of the documents, and how the company could be restructured. Elizabeth went out to the terrace and sat there while the men finalized everything. When they were finished, Nathan left and David made his way to the terrace. He offered her a glass of wine.

"It's cold out here." Elizabeth rubbed her arms but stepped away from him. David went back inside and grabbed his own coat before retrieving her designer jacket and a blanket off the back of the sofa. Snow flurries swirled around her like fairies, and he wondered why she stayed there instead of coming inside. He draped the jacket over her shoulders, and the blanket over that. She pulled both around her. Was she blocking out the cold? Or him?

It was time to come clean.

"I'm sorry for everything, Elizabeth." She glanced sideways at him but didn't speak. He cleared his throat and stepped closer. "I'm sorry for the affair, for Yuri, for the baby, for all of it."

"You don't need to say anything, David. It's in the past."

"Yes, I do, Elizabeth. You were a lonely woman, and I . . . I saw you on your rooftop. I could see the pain behind the invitation in your eyes. I should have taken steps to bring Yuri home, instead of taking advantage of his absence."

She turned to face him and put her hand up between them, but David continued.

"No, don't stop me. This is all my fault. I should have had more control. It shouldn't have mattered if you stripped naked in front of me. Well, I guess you kind of did. But it shouldn't have mattered. I shouldn't have responded. I should have respected you." He ran his fingers through his hair to keep from pulling her close.

"What gets me, what I don't understand, is that you stood up for me in that boardroom today. That was your chance at revenge, and you didn't take it. Why didn't you take it?"

Sighing, she stepped back and looked across to her terrace, again. "Well first of all, there was Pete. His words were so much like a sign, although I don't really believe in signs. But then, Leoni showed me some things about myself. I guess I had never felt truly loved. Not in a long time. You showed me attention, and it felt good. But it wasn't the kind that lasts forever, and I didn't see that until it was too late. That wasn't your fault, however. It was mine."

"I'm sorry."

"Don't be. I forgive you." She walked away a few steps before turning back. "Leoni showed me something in the Bible. About how much Jesus loves us. Something about how wide, and long, and high, and deep. That we are a part of His family. It made me feel a peace I haven't felt in a while. I didn't need revenge. I needed truth. And for what it's worth, I'm sorry, too."

He stepped forward, closing the gap but not touching her. "I had a long talk with a nice minister and his wife while I was gone. He reminded me that I am not beyond redemption. Jesus died for my sins, too. I was at my wits end. Found myself face down in a little church, thinking I was lower than the dust I was sneezing. And this man walks in and starts reading the Bible to me like he knew exactly what I needed to hear. It was strange but comforting."

"Face down in a little church? What were you doing there?" She scrunched her eyebrows in surprise.

"I rented an SUV and started driving, not really knowing or caring where I was going. I ended up in Indiana. And I found a tiny little church way out off the beaten path. Nobody was there but I felt a pull, so I went in, and well, I broke down. The minister came in while I was lying there on the floor. It was pretty embarrassing. But he knew who I was, and he was really nice. I actually spent several days there. We even went fishing together. I think I made a new friend."

Elizabeth made a small chuckle. "Except for Leoni, my only other friend is a talking bird."

"Well, God speaks in a variety of ways. Why not a bird?"

"Why, indeed?" He could see a hint of a smile from the side of her face. But he noticed she didn't include him as a friend. His heart sank, but he guessed he deserved that.

Chapter Twenty-Eight

Elizabeth groaned and rolled over in bed as her phone continued to buzz and chime. Who would be calling her at this hour? She picked up the phone, hit the ignore button, and let her hand fall to the mattress with the phone still in it. Less than a minute later, her phone was ringing again.

"Enough. All right." It was a long, emotional day. Especially since she voted against her grandfather. She knew he was not pleased with her decision.

He left suddenly after the vote, not speaking to her at all as he gathered his laptop and strode from the room. He expected her to simply sign over her proxy and be done. But her heart and conscience would not let her do that. She did the right thing. She was certain of it. But the look on his face as he left the room broke her heart.

Her phone rang for the third time. Hitting the green button, she sat up in bed to focus.

"Hello. This is Elizabeth."

"Elizabeth Yassin? This is Sergeant Stone with NYPD. I am sorry to report the death of your grandfather, Antoni Yusavi. I need you to come to the station for a few questions, please. We will be sending a uniformed officer to escort you."

"Dead? My grandfather is dead?" How can that be? "Do I have to come right now?" Her foggy brain couldn't even process what she was hearing.

"Yes, ma'am. I have Officer Fields on the way. She should be arriving at any minute, but I wanted to give you a courtesy call so that you would be prepared."

She disconnected the call and sat in silence, stunned. Her grandfather was a legend to her. He practically raised her. The kind of man that would live forever, in her eyes. Now he was gone?

Her phone chimed with a notice from the security guard downstairs. The officer was on her way up. She quickly threw on jeans and a sweater and ran a brush through her long hair. Would there be media? Probably. She dabbed on some makeup, not wanting to be seen on some tabloid post in one of those this-is-what-she-looks-like-without-makeup pictures. The knock on her door was authoritative.

"Mrs. Yassin?" The officer had one hand on her sidearm, the other holding her ID. Two other officers stood next to Officer Fields, who handed her a piece of paper.

"We have a warrant to search your apartment."

"Excuse me? I got a call from Sergeant Stone. He said my grandfather is dead and you wanted me to answer some questions. He didn't say anything about a search warrant." She opened the door wider to let the officer in.

The two men wore black nitrile gloves and pushed past Elizabeth to begin their search. They went through her cabinets and drawers. Searched under the cushions on her sofa and chairs. Stripped her bedclothes and turned the mattress over. They went through her closet, bathroom, and office. Finally, they returned to the living area with her copy of the documents from the vote, handing them to Officer Fields. The woman nodded, and the two men left the room to stand by the elevator.

Elizabeth stood still, not knowing what to say. The shock reverberated in her head. Pete ruffled his feathers from behind the cover

over his cage. She half expected him to shriek in indignation. She was surprised they had not gone through that, too.

"Please tell me what is going on. I don't understand why all of this is necessary. What happened to my grandfather?" She felt tears building behind her eyes that were still gritty with sleep.

"We can discuss this further at the station. Your grandfather was a very powerful man, and several people may have wanted him dead. We are investigating anyone close to him, starting with you."

"Investigating? I don't understand."

"Your grandfather died of a gunshot wound to the head."

Overcome, her mouth turned into a perfect O, and her hand flew to cover it. Eyes wide, she stared briefly at the officer before turning to look away. She picked up her purse and a coat and walked in silence out into the hallway. Closing the door behind her, she turned to lock it. Her brain operated on autopilot. This could not be happening.

The officer escorted her to the unmarked car that was parked next to her elevator. At least there was no chance of anyone seeing her. Numb with concern and fear, she allowed the officer to guide her into the back seat, the woman climbing in after her. She mechanically clipped her seatbelt and didn't even hear the door shut as the officer settled in beside her. The two men took the front two seats.

The drive to the station was short. That was good and bad. Good in that she didn't have time to worry; bad in that she didn't have time to think through what might have happened. She remembered that she didn't call her attorney. Should she? Would she need one? Was she a suspect? They searched her apartment, after all. It was all too surreal.

At the station, she saw another officer leading David and Nathan down a different hallway. Were they being questioned, too? What in the world was going on?

"I need to talk to David, please. And probably Nathan, too, since I didn't bring an attorney."

"You can talk with them later. Right now, we just have a few questions. Purely a formality. You are not a suspect at this point. Just a person of interest because of the circumstances."

At this point? What did that mean? She wanted to ask, but she didn't dare open her mouth. They reached a small room, and the officer waved for Elizabeth to enter. She sat in the plastic chair at a round table and looked around at the barren room. No plants, no color, no magazines to read. Cameras were mounted from each corner of the ceiling. She thought of the well-known phrase, encouraging her to smile. She thinned her lips instead.

An hour went by with no notice from anyone, leaving her to sit and worry in silence. They locked her purse away after searching her, and she wasn't permitted to keep her phone. But her watch told the time, at least. She tapped her manicured fingernails on the table. Crossed one leg over the other and swung her foot. Stood and paced when the foot on the floor fell asleep. The hour was early, and she yawned, wishing she could go back to bed. What was taking so long? Would they bring her any coffee? A bottle of water? Or had they forgotten her?

She wondered where David was, and if he was in a similar room. Why would the police think either one of them would have anything to do with her grandfather being killed? Who would hate him enough to shoot him? He was a kind man. Had a lot of power, yes. But was someone that angry with him? She took a deep breath, holding her hand to her chest. Her heartbeat was thumping hard enough to power the city.

Finally, after what seemed like waiting half the night, a man dressed in plain clothes entered the room, followed by a woman with a laptop. Elizabeth stood.

"Mrs. Yassin." The man held out his hand. "I am very sorry for the circumstances that brought you down here this morning."

Elizabeth extended her hand, and they touched briefly.

"Please, have a seat."

She sat across the round table, the woman with the laptop between them. Trying to remain calm, she placed her hands in her lap. She couldn't afford to hyperventilate. Did they have an AED in the room in case she had a heart attack? Checking the walls, she didn't see one.

"Mrs. Yassin. A cleaning crew at the Chrysler Building found Antoni Yusavi when they entered his office to clean around eleven p.m. tonight. He is your grandfather, correct?"

"Yes." She felt like that was a safe answer.

"Our initial investigation reveals he died of a gunshot wound to the head. The gun was found by his side. Do you own a gun, Mrs. Yassin?"

"What? No. Of course, not." New York laws made it extremely hard to own a gun, even if she did want one. Which she didn't.

"Our detectives are still investigating. But social media is reporting that you and your grandfather had a disagreement earlier today regarding a vote to oust David Kingston as CEO of his company. Is that correct?"

"He voted one way. I voted the other." She twisted her hands in her lap. It would not do to show nerves.

"There were others in the room that voted with you. Correct?" The detective's gaze on her was solid. Did he even blink? Her eyes were scratchy, and she wanted to rub them, but kept her hands still.

"Yes, Nathan, David's attorney. He had a proxy." The woman typed on the laptop. What kind of notes was she writing?

"And you were also asked to sign a proxy. By your grandfather?"

"Sir, if you don't mind, I don't understand what any of this has to do with my grandfather's death. And how do I know it was really my grandfather? Where is his body? I want to see him." Was he trying to rattle her?

"Our investigation is normal procedure, Mrs. Yassin. He was, after all, killed by a gunshot wound. You do want us to find the killer, don't you?"

"Yes. Of course." Elizabeth coughed, trying to get the dryness out of her throat. "May I have some water, please?"

"Certainly. I can also arrange for you to view the body, if you want to, when we finish our discussion here." The detective continued his steady gaze on her.

Nodding, she sat silently.

"You and Nathan Shepherd were seen entering the private elevator to Mr. Kingston's penthouse this afternoon. After the vote."

She stared back at the detective. Where was her water?

"It's my understanding that you and Mr. Kingston had an affair, and there was a child born of that affair that died soon after birth."

Okay. This was going off the rails.

"Should I have an attorney?"

The detective leaned forward, his eyes making full contact with hers.

"Do you want one?"

"Yes." She would not offer any more information. She knew she hadn't shot anybody, but she didn't want to say anything that might implicate anyone else, either.

"That's all for now, Mrs. Yassin. The officer who brought you here will escort you out."

That's it? What was going to happen next? All she knew was, she was tired and distressed. Who wouldn't be? She would go home, sleep until the sun was overhead, then call her attorney. But first, she had to see her grandfather.

———

The detective led Elizabeth down a long hallway, where they went through double doors and down a flight of stairs. Another long hallway that looked more like a tunnel made several twists and turns before ending at a single door.

"Where are we?" Elizabeth scrunched her eyes in confusion.

"This is the morgue, Mrs. Yassin. The tunnel we came through connects to the station we just came from, across the street. This is actually the back door.

"Oh. Okay. She straightened her sweater and prepared herself. They stepped inside the door.

"Wait here." The detective walked several feet away to talk to a man in a blue lab coat. His hair was black and hung over his shoulders in dreadlocks. Was he the coroner? They turned her way.

"Elizabeth, this is Dr. Stan Jarrett. He is the forensic pathologist on duty tonight. He will escort us to see your grandfather."

Swallowing, Elizabeth nodded. "Thank you, Dr. Jarrett."

The trio walked through another set of doors into an area that was cold. She rubbed her arms, the chill seeping through the sleeves of her sweater. Banks of drawers lined two walls. Stainless steel gurneys stood along a third wall.

"I apologize for the temperature. We keep this room just above freezing, between thirty-six and thirty-nine degrees. For reasons that I assume you understand."

She nodded again, swallowing as she did. "I can image the smell might be overpowering."

"Well, we don't want decaying bodies on our hands. That interferes with our investigations."

He stopped at a drawer marked with the number 226. Her grandfather was a number.

Opening the drawer a couple of feet, he motioned for Elizabeth to step closer. As she did, he pulled back the white sheet that covered the body.

Both hands rushed to cover her mouth, the bile rising. She gagged and spun away from the sight. No further identification was needed. Her grandfather was dead.

"Are you okay?" The doctor gave her a compassionate gaze.

"Yes. Thank you." She turned to the detective. "Can you take me back now, please?"

"Certainly, Mrs. Yassin."

She needed the water they had promised. And not delivered.

———

David and Nathan sat in a small room with a round table. There was barely enough space to move between the chairs and the walls. It was devoid of any decoration, and the air was stale.

"I'm not sure what this is about, but let me do all the talking." It was standard attorney jargon.

"All I know is, Antoni is dead, and they have questions." David sat quietly with his hands folded on the table. Nathan had a small paper notebook and ink pen. That was all he was allowed to keep. Their phones and IDs had been confiscated at the desk when they entered the building.

A female detective entered the room, followed by a male officer with a laptop. David knew that everything they said and did was being recorded, so they'd kept their conversation to a minimum while waiting. The more than two-hour wait was frustrating, but he knew that was part of their investigative process. A person under stress would reveal far more than he or she realized.

"Mr. Kingston. Mr. Shepherd. I'm Detective Rogers." The woman extended her hand, and the men shook it briefly. She was pretty. He was sure that was also designed to distract him while they questioned him.

David was shocked to hear that Antoni had been shot. He knew the meeting over the vote had not gone as anyone expected, but murder? No. He would not believe anyone would do that to his long-time friend and mentor.

"Antoni was my friend. Was he murdered? If so, I want it to be fully investigated and the perpetrator brought to justice."

Nathan laid his hand over David's and shook his head slightly.

"Mr. Kingston. This is a death investigation. It has not been ruled a homicide. We are merely asking questions."

He sat back in his chair and tried to relax.

"We received a search warrant for your premises. You will be happy to know we didn't find anything significant, and the security cameras did not show you or anyone else coming or going this evening after your attorney left. Except Mrs. Yassin. She left an hour after Mr. Shepherd. We will, however, subpoena copies of any documents related to the vote. We understand it was a very contentious meeting. They tried to vote you out."

"You searched my home? Who let you in?" David pounded his

fist on the table once, then quickly recovered. This was unconscionable. But becoming angry would not solve the problem. Someone killed Antoni, and they thought he was involved.

"We will be pursuing action for this invasion of privacy. Where is the warrant? You had no probable cause." Nathan made the threat, but David knew it was baseless. If the police had a warrant, they could do what they wanted.

"Settle down, attorney. A man is dead. We are simply doing our jobs, and most evidence is found within hours after the crime. We didn't find anything." The lovely detective glanced at her male assistant, who produced the warrant from a folder.

"Of course you wouldn't. My client is innocent." Nathan perused the warrant. "May we leave now?"

"Yes, you may leave." The detective stood and straightened her blouse. She was dressed to appeal to David's human nature, but there was no appeal there. He only wanted to see one woman. Had she also been brought in for questioning? Had they searched her suite, too? Surely she didn't have any involvement in Antoni's death. She would be in as much shock as he was.

The door opened, and another officer stepped into the room, motioning for the detective. She and her assistant left with the officer, leaving David and Nathan alone again. Nathan scribbled a note. It was a single question mark. David shook his head and shrugged.

Chapter Twenty-Nine

The next day, Elizabeth was accompanied by Nathan as she returned to the station. David was released after several long hours of waiting and interviewing. This morning, she received a call from the detective who said he had additional news. He said he would not deliver the new information over the phone, so she immediately called Nathan, rather than her personal attorney, since he was already up to speed. She knew he would represent her best interests, if needed.

Nathan held his hand on her back as they went through the sliding glass doors to the main lobby. Detective Stone met them there, and they walked down the hallway again, but this time to his office. Not the interrogation room.

He handed them each a bottle of water. She had a feeling this was not good news.

"We found a note at your grandfather's office, on a printer down the hall. It was sent from the deceased's laptop. The cleaning crew doesn't touch any of the equipment, so it was missed the first time we searched. I have requested a full autopsy." He gave Elizabeth a pair of nitrile gloves to put on, then handed her the note.

My dearest Liza. I love you with all my heart. You have been my light and joy since I first held you in my arms as a newborn. First and foremost, I want you to know that.

My doctors tell me I have an aggressive tumor in my brain and have less than a month to live. Rather than fight it, I have decided to end it. I know this will hurt you, and I am sorry.

I tried to provide for you in the best way I know how. But you have made your choice in voting with David. You are the beneficiary of my shares, and with them, you and David can run the company together. I hope he takes good care of you.

All my love,

Grandfather

Elizabeth read the note again. Tears rolled down her cheeks as she realized the importance of his words. Not only had he been dying, he thought she had chosen David over him. She voted with her conscience, and she still believed that was the right thing to do. She didn't understand why he tried to take over the company, anyway. The tumor must have affected his reasoning.

"Does this mean the investigation is over?"

"We will do an autopsy to verify the claim in the note, but if they find the tumor, then yes. With the trajectory reports and forensic evidence, we can confirm that he fired the bullet into his own head. You have my deepest condolences, and apologies for any inconvenience our investigation has caused."

"Is she free to go?" Nathan handed her a tissue.

"Yes. She is free to go."

Compassion filling his eyes, Nathan helped her stand. "David is waiting."

She walked out with Nathan, numb from what she had just

learned. Her grandfather had killed himself. She would never see him again.

———

"Welcome aboard, Mr. Kingston. It's good to have you back, sir."

"Thank you, Benjamin. It's good to be back."

"And you, too, Mrs. Yassin. It is a pleasure to serve you."

"Thank you, Benjamin. I have heard a lot of good things about you." Elizabeth patted the box that she held cuddled in her arms before handing it to the flight attendant. "These are my grandfather's ashes. Please stow them in a safe place.

The young man had kind eyes. His reddish-brown hair made the green of his gaze stand out.

"Certainly, ma'am. It will be my honor to take care of such a great man. I'm sure he was much loved."

"Yes. We all loved him." A tear threatened, and she swiped it away with her hand.

She was taking her grandfather back to Israel. She knew he would want his final resting place to be among the centuries of patriarchs before him. Jewish custom does not allow for cremation, but Antoni had left instructions for his ashes to be returned to his homeland and scattered into the wind. A second tear rolled down her cheek as she took her seat in the plush leather chair.

Looking around, she admired the décor, welcoming the distraction from her thoughts. The colors were so like David, who held her hand as the private jet rose smoothly into the air. He had made the gracious offer to escort her to Israel, which she sincerely appreciated.

They were flying overnight. Sitting by the window, her elbow on the armrest and chin in her hand, she watched the millions of lights below, their colors blending into nighttime rainbows. Times Square was off in the distance, but as they rose higher, she could still see the movements of patterns and images from the many digital screens.

The lights soon gave way to inky blackness as they soared over the ocean. Stars shone brightly above them, the Big Dipper and North Star out there somewhere. She had never been very good at finding the constellations that guided sailors for centuries. If she had to depend on them, she would be utterly lost.

The moon rose as they flew further east, smiling at them. This could be a good trip after all, in spite of the reason. She tapped her manicured fingernails on the armrest.

"Here. I have some music for you. It may help you to relax." David handed her a device that looked like a phone and some earbuds. "It's an MP3 player. Like the old school devices, but with the latest cutting-edge technology. It will hold up to eight thousand songs, so I loaded it with ten hours of music. It won't get us all the way to Israel, but it will take up most of the flight."

"Thank you, David. You didn't have to do all of this, you know." She gestured around them to the private luxury aircraft. He would have lost all of this if she had voted against him.

"Yes, I did. I owe you more than I can ever repay." He paused. "There is also a master suite in the back, if you would like to lay down and rest."

She quirked her eyebrow at him.

"I'll stay here. These seats recline and are quite comfortable."

"Okay, then. I will stay here, too." She relaxed, leaning back in her seat.

Pushing the earbuds into her ears, she found the small music player easy to use. David had loaded the same guitar track that was playing the night of their first dinner. But this time, it was different. Soothing. Peaceful. She closed her eyes and felt his hand as he placed it gently over hers, his thumb rubbing back and forth in an easy pattern. Soon, she was asleep, the mellow drone of the jet soothing her fractured nerves.

———

They arrived in Tel Aviv ten hours after departing New York. All international flights were closely monitored due to threats from

Hamas and heightened sensitivities with neighboring Arab countries. Ben Gurion International Airport was the only airport in Israel that allowed traffic from America. Elizabeth was a duel citizen, but it still made her nervous.

They circled the airport with the sun high overhead, having moved forward several hours during flight. David pointed out the window to the inverted dome, the central feature of the airport. It not only collected water, but also allowed that water to flow like a waterfall through an eyeball like structure into the terminal below. But today, it wasn't raining, so the bowl was dry.

They met her family at Terminal 3. David held the box containing Antoni's ashes like it was a precious jewel. It was, in fact, to both of them.

"Elizabeth!"

"Mother!"

They cried out together as they rushed into each other's arms. It had been several years since she had seen her family. She vowed inwardly that it would not be that long again.

She turned to see her father holding his hand out to David, and the two men shook. She wasn't sure how he would be received, but she was glad to see they were meeting on amicable terms.

"How long are you staying?" Her mother continued to hug her tightly.

"Three days. David has booked hotel rooms for us. But the company is going through a restructuring. We will need to get back by the end of the week."

Her mother leaned back, capturing Elizabeth's chin in her hand.

"No hotel. It has been far too long. You will stay with us. Both of you. There is plenty of room. And every minute will be precious." Her mother looked back and forth at them.

She glanced at David and her father, who was listening. When David nodded, she smiled. Could things be different for them now? Was there a future for them?

———

David stood by Elizabeth's side as she released Antoni's ashes into the breeze over the Dead Sea. The same sea they disagreed over regarding the Jordan deal. He wanted to build on the east side. Antoni on the west.

It was called the Salt Sea in the Bible. The lowest point on earth, it had a powerful, sulfur-like odor. Native residents didn't notice it much, but the pungent smell was strong in David's nostrils. Trying not to disrupt the moment, he coughed quietly into his sleeve.

Antoni's will requested he be returned to the home of his ancestors. David had known that for many years, as his mentor had often spoken of it. Now, his dust was in the wind, a whisp of time, mingled with the centuries of those who had gone before him.

"'The grass withers and the flowers fade away. But the word of the Lord endures forever.'" He repeated the words softly. It came from the book of Isaiah, chapter forty, and had once been one of Antoni's favorite verses. It was very appropriate today.

He harbored no anger toward his friend. A brain tumor can cause a person to do many things they wouldn't do otherwise. Change personalities. Distort memories. And then, of course, there was the affair. He hoped Antoni had forgiven him for that.

And as for the woman at his side? He realized he had fallen in love. Her strength and endurance far surpassed his own, making him feel weak-kneed. She had suffered much, losing her husband, her baby, and now her grandfather. That had not all happened at his hands, but he felt responsible for it. Yet, here she stood by his side, with no malice over anything. She also defended him to his board, providing the votes needed to retain him as CEO of the company bearing his name. Yes, she was physically beautiful. But beyond that, she thawed his heart. What would she say if he told her he was in love with her? He shook his head and held his tongue.

"Grandfather is home." Elizabeth's words were soft.

"And at peace." David gave her a quick squeeze, then stepped aside as her mother and father gathered around her with hugs. They were very gracious to him. But Antoni was their family, and this was their time to mourn their beloved. He stood quietly with his hands clasped behind his back as they huddled together, the soft breeze whispering around them.

They stood that way for several moments. Then her mother stepped back and held her arm out to him, pulling him into the family hug. He relished the warmth. Perhaps someday they could be a true family. But that would be up to Elizabeth. He wasn't sure she would ever want to be with him again. And he didn't have the right to ask.

Chapter Thirty

"So, what now?"

David turned his gaze away from the window of the SUV, looking like a lost little boy. He wore jeans for the entirety of their trip to Israel. Elizabeth thought the new style suited him. The powerful CEO was humbled by the events of the past year.

"I don't know, David. Antoni's attorney says it will take a while for the will to go through probate. But I guess everything that was his, is now mine."

"You will have a seat on the board." The soft gaze in ice blue eyes made her shiver.

"I'm not sure I want that. I would rather work with Leoni on a new fashion line."

He chuckled. "Yes, you certainly love your fashion. But I have another question."

"What's that?" Did she dare hope?

Their flight home was bittersweet. Antoni was laid to rest, his estate would become hers, and she would be a very, very rich woman. She didn't need David's money, but she had never wanted that, anyway. She would have a seat on the board because she was now a major stockholder. But she would defer to David on how to run the company. It was his. He had built it. He would rebuild it.

Carlos, his long-time driver and friend, made the way through the busy city streets as they returned home from the airport. She would never want to drive through this mess. Cars were bumper to bumper, sometimes cutting each other off with barely an inch or two between them. Freight trucks blocked lanes as they unloaded their goods. Horns blared from impatient drivers wanting to get around them. She held her breath as the SUV wove through the tapestry. She didn't know how much Carlos made as the CEO's driver, but he deserved a raise. Anyone who could navigate through this mess without so much as a single bump or scratch was priceless.

She startled from her thoughts when David's hand touched hers.

"Elizabeth?"

A look of concern crossed his face.

"I'm okay. Just nervous about all this traffic."

"I don't think it ever slows down. Carlos has been doing this for over thirty years. Put two kids through college. I trust him completely." He tapped the window between them and the driver, which was open today. "Isn't that right, Carlos?"

"Yes, sir. And you've been very generous, sir." Carlos winked at Elizabeth through his rearview mirror. She wished he would keep his eyes on the road.

Christmas lights decorated every tree and building as they made their way through the final blocks. She had all but forgotten the upcoming holiday. What was Leoni doing today? The woman had several kids and grandkids. It would likely be a happy time, with a house full of noise and love.

Home. Her home would be an empty, lonely apartment. Except for her bird. She was thankful for Pete, but he wasn't enough.

———

David escorted Elizabeth to her penthouse while Carlos took David's bags to his own suite. He had never been in her place, and it made him uncomfortable now. This was Yuri's home. David had usurped his wife. There was no justice for the situation.

He felt like he needed to ask the man to forgive him from the grave. Although that was not possible, he wanted reconciliation there, too. Elizabeth opened her door, and he walked in behind her, bringing her suitcase with him.

"Hello, hello."

"Hello, yourself, bird." David answered with a grin.

The bird was uncovered. Her maid must have been here earlier to make sure the suite was ready.

"Hello, David." The large bird's answer surprised him.

"Did he just talk to me?"

Elizabeth smirked.

"How did he know my name?"

"The maid might have said something. I think she has been teaching him a lot of things to say."

Her unseen maid. Elizabeth said the woman was in and out like a ghost, never being present when she was there. But the apartment was immaculate. Someone had taken great care.

"Hello, David." Pete squawked again.

"He's looking for a response. His name is Pete." She tugged him toward the cage that took over a full corner of the room next to the terrace doors. The giant macaw was huge.

"Hello, Pete."

The bird fluffed his wings, which were clipped when he was a chick. He had never known anything other than captivity.

"Hungry."

Elizabeth went to her refrigerator and found some pineapple chunks. Does the maid stock her shelves, too? She gave David a piece of the fruit and another one to the bird.

"Feed him. Like this."

The bird gingerly took the fruit from her hand, chomped on it, and swallowed. David followed her example.

"Thank you."

"And he is polite, too." David laughed. Elizabeth's eyes twinkled, but then she yawned.

"I have a question to ask you. But I don't want to ask it right now. Can you come over later? After you have had a few hours of rest?" He needed sleep, too.

She tilted her head at him, making him think twice about the request. Did she not want to come? Was she worried about his expectations?

"Sure. For a little while. So we can talk."

That clarified his concern.

"Six o'clock good? I'll order takeout." He didn't need to be catered to. He was a changed man.

———

David opened the door to allow the pizza delivery man to place the boxes on his table. He included salad, breadsticks, and a pastry-like dessert that won restaurant awards, the aroma filling his home. He hoped the simple fare made a statement. Elizabeth could walk the runway and appear around town in Leoni's designs. He would prefer anonymity. It was a reverse of their previous lives, but he was looking forward to it.

Ten minutes after the pizza was delivered, he received the notice on his phone that she was on her way up. He held his door open for her and inhaled as her jasmine perfume filled his senses. She was dressed simply in yoga pants and a sloppy sweater. Was she looking forward to a more laidback life, too?

His guitar track played softly in the background. Conversation between them was muted while they ate. His lights were low, but bright enough to let her know that this dinner was different. He had no expectations tonight. Well, just one. He wondered what her answer would be.

"Let's go sit down on the sofa." It was too cold to sit on the terrace. He took her hand lightly in his, and they sat down together, a foot of space between them.

"I've been thinking about this a lot." He swallowed, his nerves kicking in. He was never nervous. He was David Kingston. CEO of Kingston Holdings. And he was terrified.

"Speak your mind, David." Her voice was a whisper.

"Look. I know I don't have the right to ask this question. I don't deserve a second thought, much less a second chance. The last couple of weeks has proven that to me." He scooted a little closer and laid his hand on her arm, then pulled it away. Like he remembered what he had done.

"I can't get you out of my head. You're like a rock, taking up space."

"You're comparing me to a rock?" The look on her face was almost comical.

"I'm not doing this well, am I?" What was he thinking, anyway? He ran his hand through his wavy hair, pushing the lock hanging over his forehead away from his face.

"It could be better. But you're doing okay. I think. Keep going." She nodded her head, waiting.

He closed his eyes to recompose his thoughts.

"I don't deserve your sympathy. Or your mercy. But I would like to start over. If you are willing. We can go out to dinner Friday night. We'll find a little hole-in-the-wall restaurant that serves incredible food. Carlos will know several. He has lived in this city all his life." He stopped. She just looked at him, her brown eyes full of questions.

"After dinner, we could go to some off, off Broadway theater and catch a really bad play. Find a new actor or actress that knocks our socks off. We'll be able to say we knew them when. Make a good memory. What do you think?" He moved even closer and picked up her hand. "Is there a future for us?"

———

Elizabeth pulled her hand away and rose, moving from the sofa to the sliding glass doors that led to the terrace. The Empire State

Building was only a few blocks away. Red and green adorned the top of the building tonight. Wrapping her arms around herself, she looked off into the distance. She suspected he might ask something like this.

David wanted to make a good memory. But there was plenty of bad to overcome. The image of their beautiful baby would live in her heart and mind forever. Could she move beyond that?

Turning from the view, she saw he was still sitting on the sofa, looking dejected, like she had just rejected him by moving away. It was time to set her regrets aside.

"This wasn't a good idea. Forget I asked. I will leave you alone, Elizabeth." He lifted his hand, running his fingers over his hair. The errant wavy lock with a mind of its own fell over his forehead again as he stood and turned to leave.

"David." She captured his eyes with hers. "We can start over. If you want to."

"Do you think Yuri has forgiven me?" His sigh of relief was audible. But there was still a concern in his eyes.

"God has forgiven us. Both of us. That's all that matters." She closed the distance between them and wrapped her arms around him, her head on his chest. They would do things differently this time. But she was sure that God would bless the union.

Epilogue

"Are you ready to find out the gender of your child?"

"As long as it's healthy. That's all we care about." David squeezed his wife's hand as the doctor squirted a glob of ultrasound jelly on her rounded belly. The canary yellow diamond on her finger glinted in the light from the ultrasound screen, piercing the darkness with sparkles on the walls.

They had, indeed, gone to the off, off Broadway show and sat through a really bad play. But there was a gem in the show. Two gems, actually. The lead actor and actress were very talented and did the best with what they were given. David decided then to underwrite a Broadway play, and encouraged a producer that Leoni was doing business with to give the couple a shot. Both were now appearing in supporting roles on Broadway. The play he would help underwrite was in development.

They were married three months after Christmas, twice. Elizabeth recalled both ceremonies as the doctor prepped for the ultrasound. The first was a five-minute ceremony at the courthouse. Simple, clean, and completely private. No clerks with cell phone cameras, just the two of them and the judge, who was a friend of David. A week later they drove to Indiana. No private jet, just a road trip to enjoy each other's company. She smiled as he told her about going through the Allegheny tunnel and losing satellite reception. How it freaked him out.

Reverend Samuels married them again in Indiana. They wanted something meaningful that would commit their marriage to God. Leoni stood by her side as matron of honor, having flown in for the weekend to be there. Mrs. Samuels and David's parents were the only other people to attend.

The doctor squeezed warm goo on her belly. Holding David's hand, his warm fingers surrounding hers, she marveled at how far they had come. Their marriage in Indiana was a beautiful ceremony on a bright spring day. Easter lilies covered the hillside next to the church, mingled with purple pansies. Elizabeth's dress was a simple off-white knee-length shift, covered in lace. Designed, of course, by her friend and business partner, Leoni. The neckline was modest, and the sleeves were small caps over her shoulders. The weather was warm for early April.

A lot happened in the months afterwards. She and Leoni started a new business together after Leoni purchased her penthouse. Business was going well as everyone from Broadway stars to business tycoons and politicians flocked to them for their designs. They rented space in the garment district and hired multiple seamstresses and tailors. This was how Leoni had gotten her start, and she wanted to do the same for others.

Pete was loving his new home. David commissioned a specially made floor-to-ceiling cage for the bird that looked out the windows toward the city, with drapes that pulled close like those over a window. Her maid now cleaned both condos and was teaching Pete new words every day. He still sang off-key, like Elizabeth did, but his Italian was flawless.

Now it was five months later. She was sixteen weeks pregnant, a sign of God's blessing and restoration. The baby would be monitored closely throughout the pregnancy, but all signs were that the child was healthy, on schedule for a New Year's Eve delivery.

"Have you thought about names?"

Elizabeth gasped as the doctor spread the goo with the wand. It brought her out of her mental wanderings to the present. She looked at David, nodding at him for the final decision. They had talked about several different names. His name, David, or a version of her name, Bethel. But he wanted to go a different route, giving the baby his or her own name.

"If it's a girl, Tamara. And if it's a boy, Dawson." He tightened his fingers around hers, sending goosebumps up her arm.

"Well, let's see what we have here."

They waited together, husband and wife, as the doctor moved the wand over and around her growing baby bump. The heartbeat was strong, and David squeezed her hand.

The doctor turned the screen so they could watch the video. "Looks like all his fingers and toes are there, along with other important parts. Congratulations." The child sucked his thumb.

"His? It's a boy?" David watched in wonder as the baby turned a flip. "Did you feel that?" He wanted to lay his hand on Elizabeth's stomach, but the doctor was still working and her belly was still gooey.

"Yes, it feels like butterflies. I can't wait for you to feel him kick. That will come a little farther down the road."

"We're having a son. I can't believe it." He kissed Elizabeth with a peck, and she tugged him back for a second one. He looked scared and ecstatic at the same time. She was worried, too, but God was in control, and their son was in His hands.

———

Dawson Samuel Kingston was the next generation of Kingston men. They chose the name Dawson, a Welsh name, because it means "son of David." They couldn't think of anything more fitting.

The baby's cry filled the room as he emerged from the cocoon he had been growing in for nine months. It was a lusty cry. Loud, impatient, and absolutely beautiful to David's ears. His son entered the world face up, eyes wide open, fighting mad, ready to take on anything that life might throw at him. His black hair was full and wavy, a combination of her coloring and his waves. But his eyes were ice blue, like David's, his skin olive colored like Elizabeth's.

The nurse placed the swaddled child into Elizabeth's arms, and David hugged them from behind while the nurse took a picture. His quiver was full, and now David understood the passage Reverend Samuels read to him over a year ago. God had shown them grace and restored their relationship, building a strong family that would be an example to his company worldwide. Together, they would raise their son with honor and integrity. And let God build their house, His way.

THE REAL STORY

I hope you have enjoyed reading *House of Cards*. It is a contemporary story, loosely based on the Biblical account of David and Bathsheba, found in Second Samuel, beginning with chapter eleven.

David has a long history in the Bible. In fact, he is mentioned nine hundred and seventy-four times across nineteen books in the Old Testament and nine books in the New Testament. His story begins with his anointing by the prophet Samuel in the first book of Samuel, chapter sixteen. He was just a boy when this occurred, small in stature and relegated to tending the sheep while his brothers went off to fight for King Saul. But as a shepherd, David fought and killed a lion and a bear. He was already acquiring the skills of a warrior.

David was also an accomplished musician. When King Saul learned of David's skill, he brought him to the palace to play his lyre, a stringed instrument of that time. The music soothed Saul's soul.

The Israelites were at war against the Philistines, who had a mercenary soldier named Goliath that stood over ten feet tall. The Philistines taunted them, proclaiming that if anybody would fight Goliath and win, the Philistines would concede the battle. But nobody would agree to fight him, terrified of his size and strength.

When David was sent to the battlefield with food for his brothers, he saw the situation and offered to fight the giant. His brothers were aghast, fearful for David's life and how their father would react if he was killed. But Saul allowed the fight, offering his sword and armor. David turned them down, stating that God was on their side. With a slingshot as his only weapon, David selected five smooth stones to hurl at the giant. It only took one to knock the giant down, unconscious. He then proceeded to kill Goliath with his own sword, claiming the victory as he did. A warrior was born.

The people of Israel loved David and sang his praises as he won battle after battle. Jealous, Saul turned on David, forcing him to run away and hide from the king. But that is another story.

David eventually ascended to the throne when Saul died. God declared David to be a "man after My own heart." But David had his faults, and women were his biggest failure. He had forty wives and numerous concubines.

The Bible does not give us full insight into Bathsheba's side of the story. We don't know her thoughts, dreams, or motivations. We don't know what her relationship with Uriah, her husband, was really like. But we do know he was devoted to David and committed to serving him, even at the expense of leaving his wife alone for extended periods of time. So, while most of what I have written about her is purely fictional, I did try to capture the essence of Bathsheba as a lonely housewife.

We also don't know how long the affair between David and Bathsheba lasted. Was it one night, or many? But we do know that her body was ripe for conception, since she had just completed her ritual cleansing on her rooftop, in full view of David's palace terrace. So, it is no surprise to us that Bathsheba becomes pregnant. But it was devastating news for the lovers.

This all happened when the combined kingdoms of Israel and Judah were at war with the Ammonites. When David tried and failed to have Uriah visit his wife, he sent his men into the heat of the battle and instructed them to pull away at the last minute, leaving Uriah to be killed by the enemy. The price was high. Many men lost their lives that day, including Uriah. The guilt ate away at David's soul. But his pain had just begun.

When the prophet Nathan visited David, he made it clear to the king that God's law had been broken. As punishment, the baby carried by Bathsheba would die. David fasted for seven days, face down in the dirt, begging God to save the life of his son. But it was to no avail. The baby did not survive. Now David had the blood of two deaths on his hands. Still, the story does not end here.

The character of Antoni is based on a man named Ahithophel, who was David's key advisor and mentor, and Bathsheba's grandfather. When Ahithophel learned of David's part in his granddaughter's pregnancy and husband's death, he urged David's older son by another wife, Absalom, to overthrow his father and take over the kingdom. Ahithophel's anger was so strong, he wanted to be the one to kill David. He also urged Absalom to sleep with his father's concubines. In public. It would be a slap in the face to the king, and utter disregard for morality.

Absalom did take his father's concubines on the palace rooftop. But Absalom listened to other advisors when it came to the battle. It did not go well, and Absalom died when his famous long hair was caught in a tree, breaking the young man's neck. Ahithophel went home in shame and committed suicide.

We don't know how all of this impacted Bathsheba. I'd like to think that she had a friend and advisor who supported her during this time and showed her how to find God's grace. Her designer, Leoni, was added as a new character with this in mind. But she is purely fictional and has no Biblical counterpart.

The good news is that David did repent of his sin, and God restored David to his throne, as well as his relationship with Bathsheba. She gave birth to Solomon, who not only became the next king of Israel and is considered to be the wisest man in the Bible, but is also in the lineage of Christ.

Which puts Bathsheba in the lineage of Christ, as well.

Isn't it wonderful how God can use the most broken of people to fulfill His promises to us?

Cast of Characters

DAVID KINGSTON – King David, ruler of the combined kingdom of Israel and Judah.

ELIZABETH YASSIN – Bathsheba, wife of Uriah, then wife of David and mother of Solomon.

YURI YASSIN – Uriah the Hittite, husband to Bathsheba. Is killed in battle.

ANTONI YUSAVI – Ahithophel, David's key advisor, Bathsheba's grandfather.

NATHAN – Nathan the prophet, who called David out on his sin.

JONAS – Joab, David's general, leader of the battle against the Ammonites where Uriah was killed.

ABDULLAH – Wants Elizabeth for his harem. Inspired by Absalom.

AMMAN, JORDAN – Modern day capital city, formerly called Rabbah, capital of the Ammonites, where Uriah was killed.

JAMES, GRAYSON, THE SENATOR – No Biblical counterparts, but inspired by the insurrection of Absalom.

CHARLES HASTE – Hushai. A spy sent by David to thwart Absalom's takeover.

LEONI – No Biblical counterpart, but Elizabeth needed a friend.

ACKNOWLEDGMENTS

Many people have encouraged me as I have taken this journey as a new author. Family, friends, and colleagues have all pushed me along, telling me that "Yes, I can do this!"

To my friends at Safe Harbor Christian Church, thank you for holding me accountable for finishing this book. You would not let me quit, asked often for updates, and pushed me to create a work that honors God.

To my beta readers—Trena, Nancy, Baranda, Tiffany, Deana, Kathy, Beth, Susie, Daniel, Ray, and Patti—thank you for your brutal but honest feedback. You have helped me shape this book into a work that we can all be proud of.

To Cassandra, thank you for your experienced insight into pregnancy and the birthing process. You provided great material for the story.

To Bethany, my editor, and Emilie, my cover designer. You guys rock.

To my dear, sweet hubs, without whom I could not function, much less have time to write. You patiently stood by as ideas hit me randomly throughout the day and night, while I made "just one more note." Your encouragement and support are constant, and your expert research helped me fill in many blanks. I thank God for you.

And to my Lord and Savior Jesus Christ. It is Your grace that forgave my sins. It is Your forgiveness for my sins that allows me to tell this story. And it is my hope that this story will draw others to You. Thank You.

About the Author

Rena Bell Yeager is a mother and grandmother who loves reading, writing, and all things family. Retired after fifty years in business, Rena lives in Southern Indiana with her sweet hubs of many years. Together, they enjoy the laughter of their grandkids, rain on the roof, the sweet smell of alfalfa from their neighbor's field, and the friendship of their home church and their community.

A lover of music, Rena sings with her church worship team. She was also honored to sing backup harmony for the movie *America's Prayer*. Her experience in the recording studio was exhilarating, providing a lot of ideas and content for her next series of books, *Sing With Me, Play With Me, and Stay With Me,* coming in 2025.

Rena is a social media newbie and can only be found on Facebook at this time. Someday, her grandkids may help her move into the social media world.

You can reach Rena at contact@renabellyeager.com.

www.ingramcontent.com/pod-product-compliance
Lightning Source LLC
Chambersburg PA
CBHW022127310726

48972CB00007B/2227